Acknowledgements

I would like to thank God first for blessing me with the gift of creativity and the gift to write. I dedicate this book to my parents William Bullock and Brenda Bullock. Thank you mama for always being my strength, my encourager, my protector, my proof reader, my biggest critic and biggest fan. You've always been there for me. I could never repay you and I'm forever grateful.

Thank you Daddy for your love and support and for always encouraging me never to be just satisfied with life, always strive to be better.

I would like to thank my two amazing children whom I adore. Thank you to my fabulous five focus group. I truly appreciate you. Thanks to all my readers who had nothing but great things to say about my first book "The Secrets they kept". Thank you to my brothers and sisters. It's such a blessing to have such an awesome support system. Thank you to my designer of my book cover and my printer.

R.I.P to my grannies Lucille "Lu" Foree who taught me "sometimes you gotta raise a little hell to get a little peace", Mary "Mu" Scott Bullock who taught me to love The Lord always and believe in him. Helen Johnson "Mama" who taught me "be a lady at all times"..... R.I.P Elizabeth Bullock-Coleman "Aunt Lib" who I miss terribly, going home will never be the same ... I know their all smiling down on me.

Four Bad Bitches

by

Marsha Bullock

Table of Contents

Chapter One

Cut'n and Slicing

Cut'n and Slicing

The girls ended up going to the club where Luscious worked as a dancer. The bitch was bad, too; she practiced that shit all day and night. She even taught Chocolate and Déjà her stripper moves. Chocolate said she didn't need to learn no stripper moves, that dancing for dollars was some bullshit, that she was a straight hustler, and that if anybody was going to be doing any stripping it was going to be some nigga for her; plus, her pussy was so bomb she didn't need to do no fucking dancing. But Déjà took notes and did moves for her gentlemen friends if the situation called for it. Which meant if she was taking her clothes off, it was some serious cash involved. Hell, she lived in the Hollywood Hills; shit wasn't cheap. She was pretty good at stripping, too. Luscious said she should give up that bullshit job she had and come on and work at the "Wet Kitty" with her. Déjà told her she was out of her fucking mind if she thought she was going to quit a six figure salary to come work for some dollars. Plus, she had an understanding with the CEO of the company (he had a thang for Déjà) but shit, the way the economy was going, she might end up down there. When they entered the "Wet Kitty" strip club, they gave the club a walk-through just to check it out. They had been there before but never went in the club, just waited for Luscious outside. The club was packed with all types of people, from businessmen to old perverts to married couples. They spotted Luscious giving this Russian couple a private dance. They assumed he was Russian from the big tattoo he had on his arm that read "Mother Russia."

Luscious was dressed like Xena the warrior princess. Funny thing was she looked like a big-ass Amazon for real. She took this dancing shit way too seriously. Luscious, whose real name was Robin Marie Bennett, loved to dance and take her clothes off. She had danced in music videos. But her dream was to be a choreographer for dancers. She said that's where the

3

money was, behind the camera. Luscious stood 5'9" without heels. She was solid, thick-built like a brick house, with not a piece of body fat on her arms or back. Her ass looked like it was sculpted to perfection and her natural 36 double D cups spoke for themselves. She was dark brown in color and her face was beautiful--not a blemish (except for the tiny scar she got when she was a baby from having open heart surgery. She was born with a bad heart.). And her skin looked like cocoa butter. She was born in Louisiana but came to California when she was a teenager.

After she was done giving the Russian couple a lap dance the man gave her his card. He said he was willing to pay up to three thousand for a few hours with him and his wife. But Luscious declined. That was one of her rules; she didn't fuck her customers. She always said she was not a whore, just a dancer. *NOT A whore Im a dancer*

Chocolate, whose real name was Zira Charlene Muhammad, took the card out of his hand and said, "I'd be more than happy to replace her, but my prices are a little higher." The man looked at Chocolate standing there, the darkest of dark brown, pretty face, medium height, and nice plump fat ass, small waist. She was wearing her signature blue eye shadow, long fake lashes, and her natural hair was all over the place. She was rocking some black lace tights with rips, Daisy Dukes shorts that her ass cheeks were hanging out of, a wife beater t-shirt with no bra that you could see her small tits and nipples, and black steel toe timberlands. She looked at the man and seductively ran her tongue across her top lip. Then she flashed that perfect pretty white smile at him and he was sold. He said, "How much?" *Black still toe shoes*

She stepped up close to him and straddled him from the front. He leaned back in the chair, cupped her fat ass with his hands, and his eyes rolled back up in his head for a second. Then she slowly licked his face with the tip of her tongue, looked over at his wife and said, "Five G's for the night, cash upfront only, and I pick the location."   *5k for tonight*

The man took another squeeze of her ass. He said, "Name the place."

Chocolate said, "Let's just sit here and have a drink and discuss that."

Déjà just rolled her eyes at Chocolate. Déjà was use to Chocolate seducing men. They all had that skill, but Chocolate had a way of driving men crazy. Maybe it was the seductive, off–the-wall way she dressed or her up-front, in-your-face gangster attitude. Déjà wasn't worried about nothing happening to her because Chocolate toted a pistol in her bag and a razor blade under her tongue. She said she never knew when she was going to have to shoot a nigga or cut a bitch.   *pistol in her bag and*
Pistol chocolate

Déjà and Luscious just shook their heads and walked to the back of the club to the dressing room. When they got there they spotted one of the dancers that Déjà had a problem with. She stepped up to Luscious and Déjà. She looked them up and down and said, "When did they hire Ms. Piggy?" and pointed to Déjà and rolled her eyes. (Déjà was about 5'2", 160 pounds of pure thickness, flat stomach, small waist, round hips and ass, perfect tits, caramel brown skin, and simply beautiful. The saying was "she was thicker than a frozen Snicker").   *thicker than a snicker!*

Luscious said, "Bitch, who the fuck you talking to?"

Déjà stepped in front of Luscious and said, "I got this." She then looked

5

over at the girl. Déjà said, "Bitch, if you still tripping over Lucas, get over it" (Lucas was the girl's boyfriend who happened to have had a fling with Déjà years ago but they remained very close friends). Déjà continued to say, "He wasn't all that, but those three mortgage payments and the trip to Italy were right on time."

The girl was heated she said, "Fuck you, fat bitch."

Déjà replied, "No thank you, I don't do bitches, but if I did you wouldn't be my type because bitch, I could do better! Besides, I already fucked your man." Then Déjà said, "Now bitch, go do your job that you ain't that good at, anyway."

The girl was furious. She said, "Bitch, you can't do it; your fat ass wouldn't last five minutes and I doubt if you could even get up the pole, Ms. Piggy."

Déjà replied, "Watch me." Déjà was stubborn and arrogant, and if anybody said she couldn't do something she was going to prove their ass wrong. She walked out on stage with her street clothes on. She said she didn't need no costume because she stayed ready. When she hit the stage the crowd went crazy. The very thought of a normal everyday woman stripping sent those freaks into overdrive. She told the DJ to play something sexy. Then she broke it down to the ground with the bootie wobble, and then she hit the pole. She went up the pole, spun around, and came down into the half splits--she hadn't quite mastered the splits yet. Hell, Déjà was giving them their fantasy. Chocolate was in the front row edging her on. Since birth Chocolate was Déjà's biggest supporter. Chocolate and Déjà were cousins; their fathers were first cousins. Déjà wasn't nervous at all; she did her thing. When she stripped down to her La Perla satin and lace gold bra and panties and slid on her knees across the stage to the edge and grabbed some man's head and stuck it between her thighs, the crowd was out of control. They were screaming and throwing cash on the stage.

Déjà heard Chocolate screaming, "Bitch, they making it rain for yo' thick ass." Chocolate collected all Déjà's money and gave it to her. She kissed her on the cheek and said, "Bitch, you crazy," then she left with the Russian couple to earn her five G's.

Déjà walked over to the girl and said, "Bitch, don't ever underestimate a fat pig. We eat anything, and I just ate your ass alive." Then she dropped all her tips (which added up to a few hundred) at the girl's feet. She said, "You look like you need this more than me" and walked away. As she walked away Déjà said sarcastically, "That's that shit yo' man liked; that's why I was in Italy shopping and yo' ass was here doing whatever it is you do."

Luscious added, "Yeah, bitch." Both women exited the club. They got in Luscious's new Cadillac ERL (she was an environmentalist, but Déjà just called her a tree hugger) and rode off bumping to Too Short's "blow the whistle." Luscious dropped Déjà off at her car that was parked at her parents' house in Baldwin Hills.

Déjà hugged Luscious goodbye and hopped in her black–on–black Jaguar. She didn't go in the house because she didn't want to deal with her mother, who seemed to loathe her every since Déjà could remember. As she pulled off she saw her daddy peaking out the second story bedroom window! *Hmmm, Daddy sleeping in one of the guest rooms again,* Déjà thought to herself.

Déjà decided to drive to her good friend Chagita's house in Long Beach. Chagita, whose real name was Santiaga, was named after her dad. Chagita was the last girl of five. So since her dad knew he was never going to get a son, he named her after him and started calling her Chagita. Normally in Mexican families Chago is short for Santiago, but since she was a girl Chagita it was.

As soon as Déjà jumped on the freeway her cell rang. It was Chocolate screaming she had to cut that fool. Déjà tried to calm Chocolate down but Déjà knew when she got like that, there was no calming her down. "What happened?" Déjà asked.

"That mothafucka tried to drug me," Chocolate was screaming. She said, "I went to the bathroom after the Russian dude made a call. I left the door cracked, and then I turned on the water like I was going to wash up."

"Slow down, Chocolate, calm down," Déjà said. "Where are you?" Déjà asked.

"I'm on Crenshaw and Central, I drove down here from the airport Marriott," Chocolate replied.

"I'm on my way," Déjà said. Déjà went flying down the 405 highway. When she got to Chocolate she was all disheveled, smoking a black and mild, sitting in her Monte Carlo SS. Déjà got in the passenger side. She saw Chocolate's hand shaking with fear. She said, "Now tell me slowly

8

what happened, from the top."

Chocolate took a puff of her black and mild, then she started telling her story. She said when they got to the Marriott she started to feel a little uneasy when she saw the Russian get a big black bag out of his trunk. She said he kept receiving calls on his cell and looking around, acting strange. So she put her pepper spray in her pocket, grabbed her backpack with her loaded .22 and of course, she had her razor under her tongue. She said when they got to the room he started pulling out all these handcuffs, whips, and chains from his black bag. She immediately told them she wasn't into S&M.

He grabbed her by the throat and said, "Shut the fuck up, nigger bitch. You gon' be a good little monkey and do what I say. And right now I want my cock sucked!" Then he locked the room door.

Chocolate didn't react. She said she calmed him down by saying, "Easy big fella, if that's what you like." She said, "First let me freshen up."

Chocolate noticed that the Russian lady never said a word. She seemed to be scared of him. And by the bruises and bite marks on her body, he had been inflicting his fetish on her. She looked at Chocolate with shame and fear. Chocolate walked to the bathroom. The Russian wasn't worried about her going out the window, as they were several flights up. Chocolate peeked out the door and saw him give the Russian lady what looked like ecstasy pills. Then they poured three drinks and the man dropped some white powder in the drink that was for Chocolate. "Come on," he shouted for Chocolate to come out of the bathroom.

Cut'n and Slicing

When Chocolate opened the bathroom door she knew she had to get out because the Russian was up to no good. He instructed the Russian lady to dance with Chocolate. As they danced, the Russian lady got up on Chocolate and started rubbing all over her. She leaned in close to Chocolate like she was kissing her ear, then she whispered, "Get out of here the best way you can. He is crazy," then gave Chocolate a serious look.

Chocolate thought to herself, *Damn, what the fuck have I got myself into?*

He said, "Come dance for me, little monkey."

Chocolate walked over to him and started dancing for him. He pulled out his rather small penis and said, "On your knees, monkey."

As Chocolate bent down she positioned her razor blade with her tongue. As she went down on him, she sliced his rather small penis with her blade then she reached in her pocket and pepper-sprayed his ass. He screamed in pain. Chocolate grabbed her backpack and pulled out her .22. She pointed it at the Russian and said, ""I thought you were into pain, mothafucka." She looked over at the lady. She said, "Bitch, your husband needs help; he is a sick bastard."

The lady replied, "He's not my husband; I met him at a Russian mixer three days ago. He won't let me go."

The Russian man said, ""Bitch, I'm gonna kill you."

Chocolate put the gun in his mouth and said, "Please say something else, I

10

dare you! And what's up with this suck your cock bullshit? What the fuck are you, some kind of fucking rooster?" Then she smacked him across the face and said, "Cock-a-doodle-doo, motherfucker!"

Chocolate grabbed the briefcase of money he had; she figured he owed her the five thousand they agreed on plus a little extra for all the niggers and monkeys he called her and for asking her to suck that small baby-size penis he kept referring to as a cock. She left all the dope because she had been to prison before for possession of narcotics. She didn't want to go down that road again. She looked at the Russian woman, threw her some stacks of cash, and said, "Bitch, you coming or you gon' stay and keep getting fucked and beat to death?"

The Russian lady grabbed the cash, tossed it into her purse, and ran out of the room. Before Chocolate ran out of the room she looked down to see his baby-size penis hanging half off and he was bleeding a lot. She stopped at a payphone and called 911. She thought to herself hell, she just did that fool a favor because with that little thang, maybe they'd just chop the rest off and give him a new one. No wonder he had to kidnap bitches, because no bitch in her right mind would be okay with that. Shit, that was an instant relationship killer. Then she got in her car. She heard the ambulance coming when she pulled off.

Chocolate said, "That's when I called you" and looked at Déjà.

Déjà just sat there, stunned. She didn't say a word. Then Déjà asked Chocolate, "What happened to the Russian lady?"

Chocolate said, "I don't know; when I drove off I didn't see her."

Déjà asked her if anybody saw her come in or out.

Chocolate said no because she kept her head down, plus she had put on her long red wig. She said she was feeling a little kinky. She seemed to be calming down. Déjà knew they were going to have to call Luscious to tell her what happened, just in case he came up there. Luscious told her in French (Luscious and Déjà could both speak French. Luscious learned from her Creole mama and Deja learned from her African father, who spoke a number of languages, including French and Swahili) not to worry about it, that if that son of a bitch came near her she was going to cut the rest of his dick off. Déjà told Chocolate she was going to have to lay low for a while, because they didn't know what the hell happened to the Russian. For all they knew, he could be dead. Chocolate was looking a little worried. Déjà asked her if she wanted to report it to the LAPD.

Chocolate said, "Bitch, do I look stupid? They gone take one look at me and lock my black ass up."

They decided not to tell anybody else. The only reason they told Luscious is because she might be in danger. Déjà made Chocolate park her car in her garage. Nobody ever came to Déjà's house she didn't really have time for company. The only person that really came over there regularly was her special friend. She called him her special friend because after the break-up with her fiancé, she didn't want to be committed to another relationship. She said all men were lowdown, dirty dogs and that whatever they could do women should be able to do without being labeled a whore or slut!

Déjà was extremely bitter after the break-up. What happened left her hateful and heartbroken. She caught her fiancé cheating with some low-life trailer trash white slut. Hell, if she looked like something, Déjà might have been able to understand. Déjà found nothing about her attractive and she wasn't just saying that: she gave props where they were due; she wasn't a jealous person. The bitch looked like a wet alley cat. She looked like he had just picked her up off the streets. But that wasn't the worst of it. Not only was he cheating, he had a child. Déjà actually caught him with the woman and baby one night at a shopping mall. Normally she would have never been in that part of town; however, the particular shoe size she needed was only available at this particular mall far out in Orange County She had to drive all the way from Hollywood Hills to get them because she needed them for the event she was attending with him later on that night. She just happened upon them walking through the mall, looking at baby clothes.

Déjà couldn't believe it. She walked right up to him and said, "What the hell is going on?"

He was in shock. He stood there with his mouth open. The white girl had the nerve to ask him, "Sweetheart, who is she? Do you know her?" Then she stuck her hand out to shake Déjà's hand and said, "Hello, I'm his girlfriend and this is our daughter" and unwrapped the baby that was in the stroller.

That sent Déjà into an uproar. Before she knew it, she hauled off and smacked the shit out of her fiancé. What infuriated her most was that very morning they had just flown back from a weekend getaway to Atlantic City, spending quality time together. Déjà was pissed. She jumped on him; he was screaming, "Baby, baby, let me explain." But Déjà wasn't listening; she was whooping his ass, beating him in his head with her new shoes she had just purchased.

Before Déjà knew it, she was in cuffs and headed off to jail, where she almost had a nervous breakdown. She kept on looking around at the bars and then praying. "Lord," she said, "if you get me out of here I promise I will never do it again." She had to spend the night in jail. They charged her with assault and battery. The next morning her dad bailed her out. She went home and packed up all her fiancé's shit and poured bleach on it. She dropped it off in his office the following morning. After that they broke up. She didn't want to hear his sob story. Never again, she said, would she trust another man. If they couldn't understand that, they could kick rocks.

After their relationship was over the odd thing was her mother seemed to still want to be friends with him. She was even buying clothes for his baby girl and going on and on about how cute she was. Déjà couldn't believe it, it seemed like every chance her mother got to hurt her, she did. Déjà wondered how the fuck she could continue to be friends with that bastard after what he had done. But Déjà just said fuck both of them. Déjà had plenty of male friends and made no apologies for it. However, she did have feelings for one in particular, the one she referred to as "Mister." Déjà liked him because he had that "I don't give a fuck attitude" and he seemed like he hated everything and everyone. Plus he was fine as hell. He let Déjà do whatever she wanted; he never questioned her. But she always made time for him and he made time for her. From the beginning they had a clear understanding that they were not exclusive. Déjà never had a problem with it. However, as their relationship progressed, at times he seemed to have an issue with it, but he never said anything so neither did she.

Cut'n and Slicing

Chocolate and Déjà hid the suitcase of money in the attic. They didn't count it but judging how heavy it was, it was a lot .They went through the bag to see if Chocolate missed any of the dope, but it was all gone. They watched the news all night for anything related to the Russian but saw nothing. Luscious said the club owner hadn't called her, and normally if anybody came looking for her, he would call her. Chocolate went to Déjà's backyard to smoke her blunt and Déjà went off to sleep; however, she got none because she was worrying about the Russian possibly coming to take them both out.

Chapter Two

Getting Out of Dodge

The next morning Déjà woke up early. She was awakened by a phone call. "Hello," she said in a tired voice.

Lucas ✗

"Hey rump shaker," she heard a man's voice say. It was Lucas. Lucas was a sexy-ass Cambodian. He stood about 5'7." He worked out daily, so he was lean. He was dark in color and very handsome. And don't let the myth about Asian men having small penises fool you because he had a nice-sized penis and knew exactly what to do with it. Plus he was a charmer; he loved spoiling women and he had a thing for thick black women. He used to say all the time that once he went black, he never went back.

Lucas was a pilot. He flew international flights, which was kind of hard to believe because he was a stone-cold gangster in his earlier years, until he got busted for assault when he was a teenager. He beat up and shot his mother's boyfriend for jumping on her. They tried to charge him with attempted murder but they couldn't find the gun. So they dropped the charges down to assault. When the police came his mother hid the gun until they left. Since he was 15, he got 3 years and served 6 months in juvenile hall and the rest on probation. When he was in juvenile hall he quickly figured out that was not the life he wanted. When he got out the judge ordered him to do community service at the airport cleaning the planes. That's where he fell in love with flying. When he was 18 he had his juvenile record expunged and joined the Navy, where he learned to fly fighter jets.

He said, "I heard all about the show you put on last night. Damn, I'm just sorry I wasn't there to see it."

Déjà started laughing. She said, "Shut up, because it's your loudmouth bitch of a girlfriend that prompted me to do it."

He replied, "I don't know why you keep calling that girl my girlfriend."

Déjà said, "Maybe because she lives at yo' house?"

"Correction, she lived in one of the houses I own," he replied.

"Oh yeah, when did she move out?" she asked.

He said, "Shit, a few weeks ago; she said she was sick of dealing with my shit."

They both started laughing. Déjà said, "She finally woke up and smelled the bullshit."

Lucas said, "Damn, I get no love from you. You a cold piece of work, boo."

It didn't seem like he minded one way or the other. Déjà surely didn't give a rat's ass; she and Lucas were just real good friends. They tried the relationship thing but it didn't work. They had too many differences, plus he had a gambling problem. However, Déjà had known him since she was a child and their friendship was solid. She met Lucas when she was in elementary school. He used to live across the street from Chocolate's grandmother in Long Beach, where Déjà spent all her time since her parents were always at work.

Although Déjà's parents were African-born and raised in Africa, she was raised in America and was totally American, from what she ate to how she dressed. Déjà's dad was tall, dark and extremely attractive. The tribal markings on his face made him even sexier. He was a well-known oral surgeon. Her mother was tall and strong. Her skin was a beautiful, creamy dark brown, and she was very attractive. That was always odd to Déjà because she never thought she looked anything like her mother. But that was okay because she looked similar to her father. However, her brother looked just like both parents. Her mom was an anesthesiologist at Cedars-Sinai hospital. They both were never home so they let her spend weekends and breaks at Chocolate's grandmother's house, where she met Lucas.

After she hung up with Lucas, she woke up Chocolate. They decided to spend the day down in Long Beach at Chocolate's maternal grandmother's house. Chocolate's grandmother had raised Chocolate since she was nine. Both Chocolate's parents were dead. Her dad was killed by the rebels in the Democratic Republic of the Congo, Africa. Her mother met him while doing missionary work there with one of her best friends. After the rebels killed him and her best friend, she returned to the States. The pain of her loss led her to drug abuse. One day she was found murdered in a crack house. Chocolate's grandmother had Chocolate ever since. Hell, she practically raised Déjà. Déjà felt more love there than she did at home. She and her mother never got along, and her dad was never home.

Déjà had a big brother who was five years older. They were very close; it seemed he protected her from their mother. He always told her to stay out of their mother's way. And that's exactly what she did. When she graduated from high school she went off to college at UC Irvine, where she earned a MBA. That MBA was all her mother's idea, not Déjà's. Her dream was to go to beauty school, then open a beauty shop and do hair for the stars. Chocolate was going to do tattoos in the back. That very thought sent Déjà's mother into overdrive. She said no child of hers was doing hair for a living. She said that a hairdresser was beneath them. Déjà's mom was adamant about her going to college. Déjà's father eased it over by telling Déjà to just do what her mother wanted and that after she got her degree he would get her a beauty salon.

Chocolate never had interest in going to college; she was too busy selling dope trying to support her and her granny. But Déjà loved her no matter what she did, even when she pimped her out to start her drug-selling career. The drug supplier, who was a grown man, had a thing for Déjà, who was only sixteen. Chocolate told him that Déjà would go out with him if he fronted her some dope to get started. He jumped on the deal. Déjà agreed to go out with him until Chocolate figured out a way to rob his stupid ass for all his drugs and his money. Chocolate told Déjà to let her know when he was going to make a big drug deal, and they set him up. After he made the deal and got the money, Déjà called Chocolate and told her where they were. Chocolate, Lucas, and Luscious came there wearing masks and packing pistols and kicked the door in and robbed them. Déjà pretended to have a fit and told him she couldn't be with him anymore because of his lifestyle. They split the money equally. They still laughed about that until this day.

When Chocolate and Déjà arrived at the grandmother's house, Déjà called her friend Chagita to come over. Déjà had promised Chagita she would give her some hair extensions last night but got distracted by Chocolate's drama. Déjà and Chagita had been friends for years. They met at private school. They worked at a production company in Santa Monica. Déjà was a junior executive and Chagita was her secretary at first, but Chagita had a very thick accent and didn't communicate with foreigners very well. Needless to say, that didn't work out very well since most of the clients were foreign. So instead of Déjà letting her go, she got her a job in corporate daycare. Hell, she didn't need to speak well down there, just have lots of patience, which Chagita did. She was a natural at working with those children. Chagita went back to school and got her degree in child development; now she was running the daycare.

Chagita changed the name of the childcare center to Pre-School. She said she was not a babysitter; she was an educator. Whatever she was teaching those children, their parents loved it. Hell, she had a waiting list of children whose parents didn't even work for the company. Chagita was a fireball, full of life, which was totally surprising considering the childhood she had. She was born in a small village in Mexico. Her father was a farmer who often smuggled drugs in his fruits and vegetables for the local drug lord .He didn't do it because he wanted to; he did it because he was ordered to or die. In Mexico when the drug lord tells you to do something you do it, no questions asked.

When Chagita was 14 her Dad (Santiago) got into a disagreement with one of the drug lords over a discrepancy of twenty dollars missing from the drug money. The drug lord said that he held back twenty dollars and that he was stealing, and he had no tolerance for thieves. Her dad spoke up and said he didn't steal, and that he was an honest man making an honest living. Besides, who was he to be calling him a thief? The drug lord was furious. He ordered his men to beat Chagita's dad. Then all the men gang-raped her, her mom, and her four sisters in front of her dad. Then the drug lord ordered them all shot in the head, execution style. Fortunately, the bullet grazed Chagita's head but unfortunately, they killed all her family.

Getting Out of Dodge

The driver, who was ordered to clean up the mess, was so ashamed of what they had done he pretended he didn't see her breathing. Later that night he came back and took her to safety. He left her with a small business owner of a paper, until he could have the coyotes smuggle her to America. The driver ordered the newspaper owner to print that there were seven bodies found murdered. Then he buried the rest of her family. When Chagita was well he sent the coyotes to sneak her into America. He set her up with this nice, quiet, hardworking family in Long Beach, California, where Chagita met Chocolate and Déjà.

"Mija', what happened to you last night?" Chagita said as she got out of her Ford F150 with her Mexican flag hanging in the back window. Why she had the Mexican flag on her truck, Déjà couldn't understand. Chagita never spoke of Mexico and hadn't been back since she got to America.

Déjà responded with, "Girl, you know me. I got caught up."

"JA, JA, JA," replied Chagita in her broken English.

Her accent was so thick Déjà often had to decode what she said. Déjà often had to remind Chagita not to repeat what she said either, because one day she was definitely going to get beat up by some angry black lady. Like one time Déjà came down to the Pre-school to eat lunch with Chagita. They had a whole discussion on one little mixed boy's hair. Chagita wanted to know why the mother and father refused to cut his hair. Déjà told her they probably didn't want to cut it because they were proud of his hair being straight and all. Chagita replied they should comb it because it looked a mess. Déjà said, "You mean it's nappy?" When Déjà examined his hair she told Chagita that the boy's hair wasn't nappy but his parents did need to grease it and comb it. Déjà had no idea that later that day Chagita was going to repeat those very words to his parents. Chagita walked right up to them and said, "Mommy, I think you should grease and comb his hair. It's not nappy but does need to be combed." The parents were livid. They reported Chagita to the junior executive of that department as a racist. Thank God that was Déjà. From that day on, whenever Déjà said something she had to explain to Chagita she could only use those words with her and her friends.

Déjà always told Chagita she was too tiny to be so loud. Chagita was a little thing, about 5 feet and no more than 100 pounds, with long, wavy brown hair that she dyed blonde often. She was really cute with a lot of style, but was always complaining because she wanted to have hips, ass, and big breasts like her black friends. She was truly a hot mess. She didn't have all that body they had, but she had enough.

Déjà started working on Chagita's hair extensions while Chocolate made tacos. Déjà could tell Chocolate was still shaken up from her run-in with the Russian. They didn't tell Chagita what happened; the fewer people who knew, the better. After Déjà made Chagita beautiful, Déjà roller-wrapped Chocolate's grandmother's hair for church the next day and painted her nails. Chocolate's grandmother told the girls if they spent the night over there on Saturday, they were going to church on Sunday. They figured that was her way of telling them it was getting late.

As they ate their tacos they saw Lucas's black BMW 755 pull into the driveway. They thought that was odd since Lucas never came to Long Beach since his mom passed away. It was even odder that he had on his pilot's uniform. He looked a little worried. He walked in the kitchen and gave everybody a hug. Chagita fixed him three tacos. As he ate he started to look like he was going to faint. He said, "Déjà, let me holla at you outside for a minute."

Déjà thought he wanted to talk about her telling his stupid girlfriend he had taken her to Italy. "What's up?" Déjà said as she walked off the porch.

"Please tell me you and Chocolate didn't meet a big Russian dude last night," he said.

Déjà was shocked. *How the hell could he know that?* she thought. "Why?" she asked him.

"Oh my God," he said, putting both hands over his face. "What the fuck happened?" he said, in full panic mode by this time.

Déjà said, "Lucas, calm down. How do you even know about that?"

Lucas walked around in circles; he stopped, put both of his hands together real tight, bit his lip and closed his eyes. He said very slowly, "Beautiful, please tell me what happened. Start from the beginning and don't leave nothing out!"

Déjà could tell he meant business. She began to tell him what happened, until she was interrupted by Chocolate's grandmother, who burst out the screen door shouting. She was pointing and looking up on her two-story house at the roof. She was screaming, "Get yo' stupid ass down."

Chocolate's uncle had gotten high on sherm (which is a cigarette dipped in

PCP) and robbed the people down the street, and the neighbor called Chocolate's grandmother when she saw him up on the roof. When he saw Chocolate's grandmother he told her to kick back because he was securing the perimeter. All of a sudden they saw this black car come flying around the corner, burning rubber, with its lights off. Chocolate's uncle shimmied down the storm drain off the roof. When the car got closer, the back door swung open. Then the uncle did a swat roll and dived in the back seat of the car. The car sped off down the street, burning rubber, with the back door still hanging open.

Chocolate's grandmother was furious. She ran out in the middle of the street, took off her house shoe, and threw it at the back of the car. She was screaming, "Don't bring yo' black ass over here no more, little ignorant bastard."

Everybody was just standing there with their mouths hanging open, staring.

Lucas said, "See, that's that dumb shit; that's why I don't come down here."

Chocolate ran and got her gun. She said she was going to find his stupid ass and shoot him for upsetting her granny. But Lucas told her to settle down because she had way bigger problems than her dope-fiend uncle. "Besides," he said, "you ain't never going to catch a dope-fiend; they too fast."

Chocolate cracked a smile, then she said, "But what are you talking about we got bigger problems?"

He said, "Just tell me what happened with the Russian, please."

All the girls sat in his BMW while Chocolate told Lucas what happened. He then said, "That Russian is a big-time dealer. I first met him on a flight from Russia. We gambled and drank. He asked me where some hot bitches were. I told him to go over to the Wet Kitty. I knew he would like Luscious." He continued, "I didn't know he was a freak, I swear. I'm so sorry. I gotta get you guys away from here until he leaves."

Chocolate said, "Did the police show up?"

Lucas said, "Yes, but they just dropped him off at the emergency room. He told them some crazy hooker attacked him and stole his money. Once his private jet leaves, he probably won't come back; however, he is pissed about his dick. They had to sew it back on. Who knows if it's ever going to work again?" Lucas said he had to get them away from California for a few days, until the Russian went back to Russia. Lucas said he was going to a pilot training in Mexico City, Mexico. He said they could hide out there until he was finished and that they could just consider it a free vacation, all on him.

The girls weren't excited. They thought, *Who the hell wants to go to Mexico?* Hell, they lived in California; it was full of Mexicans. They were practically in Mexico, but they knew it was safer from them there. Chagita was a little apprehensive, as she hadn't gone back to Mexico since her parents and siblings were murdered.

Lucas assured her she would be fine; besides she had been out of the country more than a few times. He said the passport that Déjà's dad had gotten Chagita was solid. Lucas said they had to leave on the last plane that night, which was midnight. They only had a few hours to pick up Luscious and hop on the plane. The girls insisted that they needed more time and that a few hours was not enough time to pack. Lucas said it was either get on the plane or die. All the girls looked at him like they were going to cry. He said, "All new clothes, on me."

With that said they hopped in their cars to drive to Luscious's house. They had to pick her up on the way to the airport. When they got there the screen door was unlocked and the door was halfway open. All the girls and Lucas walked in. They saw Luscious stark naked on the couch with her head laid back and eyes closed, moaning. As they got closer they saw a man's head between her legs. They all were just standing there looking, then Déjà said, "Umm, excuse me."

Luscious didn't budge but the man jumped up. Luscious said, "It's okay, those are my people." Then she started introducing them one by one. She never put on anything to cover up; she was just walking around talking naked. The man was worse: he was trying shake all their hands naked, but they all declined. Hell, his face was just between Luscious's legs; God only knew where his hands where. He was just standing there with no shame, dick hanging and balls swinging. The girls had to admit he was a gorgeous white boy: about 6 feet tall, dark hair, sky blue eyes, nice tight abs and he wasn't too bad below the waist.

Déjà wasn't really paying attention. Shit Luscious was half naked daily and nothing she did shocked Déjà. Besides, Déjà hated going to Luscious's house because of all the voodoo shit Luscious believed in. She had a voodoo doll for everything and believed in spells and all that type of weird, way-out bullshit, which made Déjà a little nervous at times. She didn't want to fuck around and go to hell. God might get pissed off about some of the shit Luscious believed in. Even though they were good friends, they were all different religions. Chagita was Catholic, Déjà and Chocolate were supposed to be Muslim/part-time Christians, depending on whose house they were at, and Luscious was into voodoo. She got highly pissed if you questioned her about it.

Luscious was always a little strange but after the break-up and the abortion she had, she was even stranger. Luscious was 19 and in college; she was a double major in dance and design. She fell in love with Déjà's brother, who was going to USC studying to be a doctor. She learned she was two months pregnant when he went off to Cornell medical school. She made the mistake of confiding in Déjà's mom, who tricked her into getting an abortion. She convinced her that her son would not be able to complete his medical training if she had the baby. She said he would drop out of medical school and get a job. Luscious felt bad; she didn't want to ruin his life. So she went with Déjà's mom to the abortion clinic. Little did Luscious know Deja's mom paid the doctor to fix her so she couldn't have any more babies. When Déjà's brother found out he was devastated. He told Luscious she should have confided in him and asked her how she could kill his child. He told her he never wanted to see her again. Nothing she said changed his mind; he even stopped speaking to his mom for a few years. Their mother convinced him she only was looking out for his best interest. However, she told Luscious after she got the abortion that no son of hers would ever marry a dancer. Furthermore, he was too good for some trash from New Orleans.

Lucas finally said, "Damn, can you guys put some fucking clothes on?

Getting Out of Dodge

Don't nobody want to see all that."

Luscious was an exhibitionist. She loved walking around naked and having people look at her. She got a big thrill out of it. However, she didn't want to be touched.

After they explained the situation Luscious was visibly upset. She said she couldn't possibly go to Mexico; she had way to much stuff on her calendar. Luscious said she had an opportunity to create a music video with substance. She always complained that videos now days didn't have a message, just girls' asses shaking and a lot of alcohol and cars. She went on and on until Lucas said he was paying for everything; only then was she was ready to go. Lucas said he wasn't tripping because he had won a large amount gambling last week in Paris, France. The girls got lucky; they got first class seats on the first flight. This was the best standby trip they had ever made. Normally they had to wait or either go on separate planes.

On the plane Déjà noticed Chagita drinking heavily. Chagita was scared to death about being in Mexico. When the plane landed they took a car to this little town called Xochimilco. It was a tourist attraction town. Lucas said there was no way in the world the Russian would even think of looking for them there. Lucas said he put in a request with one of his contacts at the airport to be notified when the Russian left the country. He told them to get some rest and he would meet them by the pool for a late lunch. He left his debit card with Déjà. He told her not to go crazy with the shopping. He gave her a budget and left for his training. The girls slept for a few hours then were off to shop. After they had overspent way past the budget Lucas gave them, they got dressed to have a late lunch by the pool.

31

All the girls bought bathing suits and wraps. They wanted to be cute sitting by the pool.

Luscious told them to go ahead; she would meet them downstairs. The girls all went to the pool and ordered drinks, then Lucas finally showed up. Déjà thought to herself he looked damn good in that black tailor-fitted Armani suit.

Chagita was finally starting to relax after Lucas told her they were thousands of miles from where she grew up; besides, that old drug dealer man was probably dead by now. Chagita spit on the ground and said, "To hell with him. I hope he's rotting in his grave."

Déjà noticed that all the women seemed to be frowning and pointing at something, or more like somebody. Déjà said, "Look at this retarded bitch" and pointed to Luscious. As Luscious walked toward them, Lucas and the rest of the girls' mouths dropped open. Luscious had on rhinestone pasties barely covering her nipples, a string bikini bottom which consisted of a very thin piece of string with a tiny flap barely covering her vajaja, and some five inch Rhinestone red bottoms.

Chocolate smiled and said, "This bitch is ridiculous."

All the women at the pool were grabbing their men and leaving. Luscious sat down at the table. When the waiter asked her what she wanted to drink, she told the waiter to bring her "sex on the beach." He could hardly write for staring at Luscious. Déjà could tell she was getting a big kick out of everybody staring at her. One man walked by and said something sexy to her in Spanish. Lucas looked at Luscious. He was furious. He said, "Is this what you call discreet? What the fuck? I got co-workers staying here." Then he shook his head and said, "What the fuck, they gon' think I'm some fucking pimp, here with all my ho's."

All the girls started laughing. Then Déjà said, "At least you got four bad bitches."

They decided to go on a tour boat after they ate, but first Luscious had to put on some clothes. Luscious reached in her bag and pulled out some shorts and a tank top. After she had got all the men aroused, she was really feeling herself.

Chocolate pointed her fork at her and said, "Bitch, you need help."

Chagita said, "No, she needs Jesus."

They all started laughing. Deja spotted a nice-looking gentleman checking Chagita out from head to toe. Déjà said, "I think you have an admirer" and glanced over at the man. When Chagita looked at him she stared for a while. Déjà said, "Do you know him?"

Chagita looked puzzled. She said, "No, I don't think so, but I feel like I know him."

As they discussed the man he approached them and said, "Hello ladies, are you enjoying your vacation?"

Déjà smiled and said, "And what makes you think we on vacation. What, are there no beautiful black women here in Mexico City?"

Déjà and Chagita started laughing. He looked confused by what she had said at first, then he said in his perfect English, "Are you making fun of me?"

As they spoke Déjà noticed that he seemed to be studying Chagita's face as if he had seen her before, it seemed like he wanted to say something besides small talk. During their conversation a group of priests walked by wearing their long robes and hoods. The priest in the back was pulling an oxygen tank. When Chagita saw him she froze with fear. She grabbed Déjà's arm and the look on Chagita's face was one of pure horror. As he walked by he took off his hood and glanced at Chagita as if he had seen a ghost. Déjà didn't know what the hell was going on. She looked at Chagita and asked, "Are you okay?"

Chagita didn't answer; she was in a trance, as if she was in deep thought. Déjà looked down at her feet to see that she was standing in a puddle of urine. Chagita had urinated on herself in fear. *What the fuck*, Déjà thought. She grabbed Chagita's face and said, "What is wrong with you?"

Chagita had tears rolling down her face. She was shaking in fear and couldn't speak. The man they were speaking to before the priest walked by stood in front of Chagita and said, "Don't look at him."

Déjà pushed the man away from Chagita. She said, "Get off her. Who the hell are you?"

The man replied, "Please miss, I mean you guys no harm; I'm only trying to protect her like I always have."

Déjà looked puzzled. She said, "I don't know who the fuck you are or what the fuck you want, but you don't know either one of us and we most definitely don't need your help."

He responded, "We have to get her out of here; she is in danger."

At that time the entire group walked over to see what the hell was going on. Lucas walked up to the man and said, "Get the fuck out of here."

By that time Chagita was crying uncontrollably. Déjà was trying to calm her down but was unsuccessful. Chagita was just standing there looking at the priest walk away. After they got her back to the hotel room, Déjà put her in the shower and kept watch on her. Déjà was getting worried because Chagita was not speaking at all. Déjà gave Chagita a shot of tequila. It seemed to calm her down a little. However, she still wasn't talking.

That night she refused to go back out and insisted everybody stay with her. She even went as far as to demand Déjà sleep with her like she did when they were teenagers at sleepovers at Chocolate's house. Déjà stayed up all night and watched Chagita while she slept. Chagita cried out in her sleep, like she often did when they were teenagers. She tossed and turned the entire night. The next morning when the girls awakened, Déjà found Chagita in the corner crying. Déjà walked over to her and sat down beside her. Chagita put her head in Déjà's lap and cried.

Déjà said calmly, "Sweetie, if you don't tell me what's wrong I can't help you."

Chagita looked up at Déjà and said, "The priest we saw yesterday?"

Getting Out of Dodge

Déjà said, "Yeah, what about him; do you know him?"

"Yes," Chagita replied. "I will never forget his face as long as I live. He raped me, my mom, and my sisters, then he allowed his men to do the same, then he ordered my entire family killed."

Chapter Three

Mysterious Stranger

Mysterious Stranger

Déjà was shocked at what Chagita had just told her. She put her arms around Chagita and said, "Sweetie, do you understand what you just said? You said the priest raped you and your mom and sisters, then ordered all of you guys killed. Why would he do that? He is a man of God; maybe you have him confused with someone else?"

Chagita jumped up and started speaking fast in Spanish. She was rambling on and on. Déjà didn't understand what she was saying; however, she clearly understood the English curse words Chagita added in every other word. Déjà didn't try to calm her down at all. Déjà let her ramble for at least an hour. Chagita finally calmed down and fell asleep on the floor. Déjà didn't even try to move her; she just stepped over her and went on with her day. After Déjà showered and got dressed, she noticed she had missed several calls from Mister. *Damn*, Déjà thought to herself.

Déjà picked the phone up to call him back but Lucas walked in the room. "Hey beautiful, what's going on? I got some good news: I got word that the Russian left the states. So whenever you guys are ready to go home, it's cool." Déjà smiled at Lucas she said, "Thank God, because this bitch is losing it" and pointed to Chagita, who was still lying on the floor sleeping. From the looks of it she was having a terrible dream: she was screaming and moving around. Déjà was going to wake her but she decided against it because Chagita needed to rest and she damn sure couldn't get on the plane tripping like that. Hell, TSA agents would have her ass in a straitjacket. Déjà told Chocolate and Luscious what Lucas said, then she decided to go eat by the pool and have a swim before they left. Shit, the way Chiagita had cut up all night and all morning Déjà felt like she needed a drink and it wasn't even noon.

Mysterious Stranger

Déjà had never known Chagita to flip out like that, and she was really worried about her. Why would she accuse a priest of raping her and her family and be so adamant about it? Déjà knew the story all too well, and Chagita never mentioned a priest, just a drug dealer. Then Déjà thought about the strange man at the pool. Why would he say he had always looked out for Chagita? As far as Déjà knew Chagita didn't have any family left and the people she grew up with where just some random people who adopted her from Mexico. Or were they? What if they knew more about Chagita's past than they had said?

Chocolate decided to join Déjà for lunch by the pool. As they left the room and headed toward the elevator, they noticed a man sitting in the sitting area at the end of the hallway smoking a cigarette. As they got closer they noticed it was the same man from the pool. "What the fuck?" Déjà said. She walked over to him.

Chocolate grabbed her arm and said, "Remember, we not in America., Watch what you do and say. We would hate to end up in a Mexican jail or worse, somewhere deep in Mexico as a sex slave, and you know they love thick black women."

Déjà started laughing and said, "Ok, but why is he following us?"

"I don't know," Chocolate replied, "but let's find out."

As they approached the man, he stood up to greet them. He stuck out his hand and said, "Good morning, lovely ladies. How are you doing this morning, Déjà and Chocolate? How is Santiaga (Chagita)?" Then he sat back down.

Déjà replied, "How do you know our names? I never said them yesterday, and speaking of names, we never caught yours, mister--and why are you following us? I don't know about Mexico but in America stalking is a crime."

He smiled at Déjà and said, "Always the fire ball. Sit down with me; let's talk."

"Naw," Déjà replied. "I'd rather stand and if you don't tell me who you are and what you want, I'm going to go to the authorities here and tell them we are scared of you."

He said, "You never have to be scared of me. I've known all of you girls since you were teenagers." Then he pulled out a photo of all of them at a party at Chagita's house.

That gave Chocolate the creeps. She said, "Who the fuck are you and why are you carrying pictures around of us when we were teenagers? What are you, some kind of freak?" She grabbed Déjà's hand. "Let's get the fuck out of here; this is some bullshit."

He stood up and said, "Please let me explain--please."

Chocolate was livid. She said, "Motherfucker, you better start talking some real motherfucking talk or we out."

He sat back down and said, "Please calm down. Sit down let me explain myself. First of all, my name is John Paul. Years ago when I was just a boy, no older than seventeen, I was a driver for a very bad man. One night that man and his gang of thugs raped and murdered an entire family. I was ordered to clean up the mess and make it go away. As I was doing that, I noticed one girl was still alive."

Déjà took a deep gasp and said, "Oh my God, you are the man Chagita never saw but always talks about how you saved her life."

Chocolate looked at him and said, "Why did you do that?"

"Because it was the right thing to do," he replied. "I sent her to America. I set her up with a good family. I never thought she would step foot in Mexico again." He said, "I beg of you to leave at once."

"And the priest we saw yesterday--the one Chagita swears killed her family--who is he?" Déjà asked.

He replied, "He is very dangerous, very dangerous." He stopped talking when he looked up to see Chagita standing in the hallway, close enough to hear his every word.

With tears rolling down her face, she charged at him, screaming. She started beating him; he didn't lift one hand to defend himself against her. Chocolate and Déjà pulled her off him. Lucas came flying down the hallway to see what was going on, and security was getting off the elevator with their weapons drawn. When security rounded all of them up, they lined them against the wall and asked John Paul in Spanish what was going on. After John Paul began to speak the security seemed to recognize him. In a panic, they started apologizing and asking him if there was anything they could do for him. Déjà was holding Chagita up at this point.

Déjà thought Chagita was truly losing her mind. When the security walked away, Lucas asked John Paul what the hell was going on.

They decided that talking in the hallway was not a good idea so they went down to the pool to eat. Lucas insisted on being in an open space at all times. At lunch John Paul retold his story while Chagita listened in horror. He said after all that happened the man who ordered his men to kill Chagita's entire family went crazy and killed all his men and disappeared. Yesterday was the first time he had seen him in over twenty years and why he was in Mexico City posing as a priest he didn't know, but he was going to get to the bottom of it. He said when he had more information, which would be soon, he would share it with Chagita.

Déjà was very skeptical of his story. She could tell he was lying and leaving out a lot.

Chagita looked at him with tears in her eyes. She said, "Did you rape me, too?"

There was an awkward silence. He said, "No, I never touched you, your mom or your sisters. I was in the car the entire time. I only came in when I heard gunfire, and then I was given the job of disposing of the bodies--and the rest you know."

"Where are they?" Chagita asked.

John Paul replied, "Does it really matter? They're all together in a grave far away from here."

"Take me to it." Chagita insisted she be taken to the grave site at once.

John Paul tried to explain to her that it was very dangerous to do that, but Chagita wasn't taking no for an answer. He told them it was a three-day drive from where they were to the grave site. Chagita said she didn't care if she had to walk there; she wasn't leaving without seeing the graves.

Lucas refused to drive through Mexico for three days. He had John Paul charter a private jet, and he flew them to the small city where they were buried. It took a lot of convincing for the rest of them to go. Hell, they didn't know John Paul and the only thing they did know about him was he was some kind of killer/hit man. Either way, he was not to be trusted. But since it was Chagita who was stirring up all the drama they said a prayer and tagged along. Neither of them was very happy about it.

When they got to the small town, Chagita seemed to remember it. She remembered playing there as a child and going to school. She insisted they go to the old farm, which was still in good repair. John Paul had taken care of it all these years. Although she didn't know the people in the farm house, he told her they were her relatives of her mom's. However, she wasn't to mention that because they all thought she was dead.

They arrived at the small graveyard. He led them to their graves all with crosses, headstones, and angels, lined up all in a row from oldest to youngest, and to Chagita's surprise there was a headstone that read, "Here lies Santiaga Ramirez, beloved daughter and sister." When she read that she burst out in tears. She fell upon the graves and wept uncontrollably. No one tried to stop her or comfort her; they let her cry as long as she needed to. This was long overdue.

On the plane ride back John Paul got a call. Then he said, "When will you be leaving for the States?"

Lucas replied, "As soon as we land this plane."

"Good," he said. He looked at Chagita. "Please never speak of this again and never come to this place again."

"No fucking problem," Chocolate blurted out.

"Why?" Chagita replied. "You know where he is, don't you? I saw you talking on your phone, so tell me where he is."

Déjà knew by the look in Chagita's eyes she wasn't going to give up, even if she dragged her on that plane back to the States and confiscated her passport. She knew she would find a way back. She was going to find that gangster who killed her family, one way or the other. Déjà discussed the situation with John Paul. She said, "I don't know why I trust you. I just do. My gut feeling tells me that you're dangerous but for some reason not a threat to us. For some odd reason I trust you."

"As you should, my friend," he responded, "but I'm not taking her to this man because unlike me, he is a threat to you and your friends."

Déjà looked over at Chagita, who was looking crazier than usual, and said, "Good luck explaining that to her!" Déjà said, "But let me add this: if anything happens to my friend, you not going to have to worry about some priest because it's going to take The Lord Jesus Christ himself to keep me off your ass!"

Mysterious Stranger

John Paul smiled. He said, "Anything less would be unacceptable."

By the end of the plane ride the girls were back on their way to the States and Chagita was driving off from the runway in a limousine Escalade with the familiar stranger they'd come to know as John Paul.

Chapter Four

The Video Call

The Video Call

Back in the states after Déjà hung up the video call with Mister, she reflected on their conversation; it did seem brief and rushed. Or maybe he just wanted to show her that he could finally get the video calls right. Or maybe he was just showing off one of his new electronic gadgets he loved so much. He was a show off. He enjoyed flaunting his success. Déjà didn't mind; it was sort of sexy. Here is this young man coming from the bottom, now having anything he ever wanted and doing it all legally.

Thirty minutes later she received another call from him. She realized it was just one of his pocket calls, except this time it was a video call. She started to hang up but a woman moaning got her attention. As she observed the video call more closely, it seemed that she was looking at a woman having oral sex with Mister. Déjà continued to observe the situation. Then she realized she was looking at it through the reflection from the mirror above the bed. She started looking around the room at what she could see. All she really could see was the bed, the people in the bed, and the night stand with a picture of what looked like a wedding. She quickly made out the images in the photo: it was Mister and the woman who was pleasuring him. Déjà was getting emotional. She started talking to herself as Mister and the woman who apparently was his wife started having sex missionary style.

"Ain't this a bitch?" she said to herself. She put her phone on mute so they couldn't hear her but she could hear them. She continued to watch; they paused for a second as they heard voices. The voice said, "Y'all started without us?" and gave a chuckle. Then a couple joined them in their bed.

"Un-fucking believable" Déjà said out loud. "Fucking freaks; this is why this motherfucker is always asking me do I think this bitch and that bitch is cute!" She recognized the other man; it was one of Mister's business associates. Déjà never liked him; he was always saying sexual slurs to her. Now Déjà knew why. She said to herself out loud, "Motherfuckers was trying to groom me for this bullshit." *Never in à thousand years,* she thought as they continued their orgy. Mister placed the lady in a doggie style position, as did the other man with his partner. Both men proceeded to have anal sex with the ladies.

As Mister's partner was moaning and groaning and telling him how good it was, she looked down to see Mister's phone on video chat and Déjà's face in the corner of the screen looking back at her. Somehow that excited her more. Déjà tried to just shake it off as a lesson learned. She didn't want to make a big deal out of it and get all emotional. Besides, when the wife realized that someone was watching, she did the most bizarre thing. She bent down closer to the camera, shook her fake breast implants, blew Déjà a kiss, then stuck up her middle finger and continued their orgy! Déjà was lost for words. What kind of freak bullshit was this? This bitch knew she was watching and didn't flinch. Déjà wasn't shocked and even madder at what was taking place. She was pissed because he lied about being married. Then she thought, *Hell, he didn't lie; he just never bothered to mention it.*

Déjà wanted to hang up but curiosity got the best of her. She had to see how this shit was going to end. And since his wife knew she was being watched, she gave a performance worthy of an award. When it was all done Déjà just shook her head and said, "Fool me once, shame on you but fool me twice, shame on me."

The next morning she got a text from an unfamiliar number. It read,

The Video Call

Hello bitch,

This is his wife! Yeah, that's right, his wifey. So I guess you caught an eye-full. That's just how we get down, but you really ain't seen shit. I've known about you from the beginning. We don't keep secrets. However, for some reason your high society ass has been off the menu. Which I can't understand anyway because you ain't all that. Bitch, you could never be me or do the things I do. So stay the fuck away from MY husband and get your own. Checkmate, Bitch.

Signed,

His Wife

Déjà was furious for a moment. She started talking to herself. "Simple bitch," she said. Then she stopped herself. She saved the message, then shook her head smiled to herself, and said, "Pitiful bitch." She and Mister were only friends with benefits. At least that's what she kept telling herself. So if that was the case, she asked herself, why was she curled up like a baby on the floor, crying over a man that she was just friends with? She started talking to herself again. "I can't fucking believe all this is happening to me! What the fuck did I ever do to anybody to deserve such a fucked up life?" She looked up to the sky, tears rolling down her face, heartbroken over what she witnessed last night. She started bawling and said, "This is what I get? This is your fucking will for me--to be fucking miserable? What kind of God are you that you let bad things happen to good people?"

Déjà continued to cry and reflect on all her life's bad experiences. She thought about all the times she'd felt God had failed her. She lay there on the floor for hours, until she had nothing left in her. She relived all the horrible things she had ever done since childhood, like that time they stole money out of the offering at church, all the little white lies she had told over the years, every rotten, distasteful thing she had ever done. Yet she still could not reflect on anything that she had ever done that would require the good Lord to punish her in such a manner. The only grave sin she could rationalize in her mind was her sleeping around.

As she lay there in all her self–pity, her cell phone was ringing off the hook: Calls from Chocolate, Luscious, and of course Mister, who was the source of all her pain at this moment and at the very top of her fuck-you list. Déjà didn't even bother to read the text or listen to the messages. She just went downstairs, cracked open a bottle of wine and cranked up her stereo as high as it could go and listened to all the man-hating songs in her iPod. She fell asleep listening to Mary J. Blige's "I'm not gon' cry" on repeat.

The next morning she decided that her pity party was over. She apologized to God for being disrespectful and thanked him for the life she had. She showered, got dressed, and turned on some gangsta rap to get herself out of the slump she was in. She erased all Mister's voice and text messages without reading or listening to one. She felt anything he had to say was irrelevant; besides, his video call said it all. She looked at herself in the mirror, standing there looking absolutely beautiful. She shook her head, pointed at herself, and said, "So beautiful yet so dumb." She picked up her phone to call Chocolate but got distracted by a knock at the door. She thought it had to be one of her neighbors maybe complaining about her forgetting to turn off the sprinklers.

As she got closer she could see Mister. *Damn*, she thought, *for this to be a gated community a lot of people get through.* She took a deep breath, then opened the door to let him in. She said, "Whatever you want to say is irrelevant; your wife said it all." He stood in the doorway for a second. Déjà looked at his face and clothes. Déjà assumed by all the scratches on his face and neck he had been fighting. She was willing to bet he had been fighting with his wife.

He said, "I'm so sorry about all this. I never wanted you to know about her or even see her."

"Then maybe you should be more careful about who you video call" Déjà blurted out. As they began to speak, Déjà could tell he was truly sorry. He explained that he married her when he was young way before he got drafted to the league. He said that he had no prenuptial with her and that if he ever divorced her, she was going to take half of everything he had. He said that they barely spoke and that if he wanted to see his daughter he had to spend time with her first. He continued to say that she was a money-hungry whore who had all kinds of incriminating evidence on him, so divorcing her was not an option. He said they lived separate lives because he no longer wanted to be a part of her sexual habits.

Déjà didn't say a word; she just listened. He said when he met Déjà he wanted her all to himself, which caused a problem between him and her that ultimately led to their separation. He said that when he found out about the video call he exploded and in a moment of rage he smacked her.

Déjà stepped back and said, "You didn't kill her, did you?"

He looked Déjà up and down and said, "Your pussy is good, but not good enough to be killing bitches over."

The Video Call

Déjà grabbed her heart and sighed with relief, then she started cracking up at what he said. They both started laughing. He said, "I mean, that would be a little extreme, don't you think?"

Déjà walked into the kitchen with Mister behind her. She said, "You know I don't have many rules, but dating a married man is one of them. I don't date married men, no matter what. Someday I'm going to be married. You know what they say: 'You reap what you sow.'"

Mister tried to talk her into continuing the relationship but it was useless; her mind was made up. That relationship had run its course, and it was over. He told her if she ever needed him he was just a phone call away. He smiled and said, "But don't video call me, because I'm blocking that bullshit from my phone."

They both laughed and she walked him to the door. She gave him a hug goodbye; she couldn't help herself and if it wasn't for the visual she had in her mind of him with his wife, she would have given him some goodbye kisses but decided against it. As he drove off she noticed an unfamiliar car parked on the opposite side of the street.

Déjà gathered her thoughts together, put aside her personal life and attended to her business. She had a very important meeting this morning with her international business associates, which meant a whole lot of negotiating and translating, both of which Déjà surely wasn't in the mood for. Normally Déjà was great at negotiating and compromising; however, after the recent events in her life she was drained of energy. Unfortunately, her secretary had set this meeting up months ago and since they were coming from out of the country there was no way to reschedule.

That would just be straight out rude, not to mention extremely bad for business. Déjà said a prayer before getting out of the car.

"Lord, please give me the strength and the patience to get through this meeting. Please grant me wisdom and clear vision to see through the lies and deception my associates are trying to get away with. Lord Jesus, please watch over Chagita in Mexico and give John Paul the strength to deal with her. Lord, please give me the strength to stay away from Mister. In the name of Jesus I pray, Amen."

As Déjà grabbed her briefcase she thought about taking a leave of absence. She had a lot going on and focusing on work was getting harder and harder. Besides, she had saved a large sum of cash over the years for a rainy day and hell if it wasn't pouring down raining right now, she thought. As she made her way up to the forty-first floor to her corner office, she heard vacuuming. She thought nothing of it because it was early in the morning. When she got to her office, as usual her secretary was there before her and waiting for her with the morning reports and a cup of coffee, and with anticipation of Déjà complaining of a headache before and after the meeting, he handed her two extra-strength aspirin.

Déjà looked at him, smiled, and said, "What would I ever do without you?"

He replied, "Child, let's both pray you never have to find out," then he gave two snaps in the air and sat behind his desk. He said, "Miss Thang, your 8:00 am meeting will be in your office shortly; they just checked in downstairs."

The Video Call

Déjà hurried in her office, popped her two aspirin, and then did a quick mirror check. She briefly reviewed the file and sat behind her desk and waited for her associates. Just like her secretary said, they were walking in the door looking like a pack of hungry wolves waiting on the prey to slip up and make a mistake. As the meeting progressed, Déjà heard vacuuming again, but this time it was right outside her office door. Déjà asked to be excused for a second so she could tell the janitor to please come back later. When Déjà asked her secretary to politely ask the janitor to come back later, he informed her that he would not be asking that wicked heffa anything. Déjà couldn't believe he said that but didn't have the time or energy to even ask him why he said it. Déjà just figured he probably had gotten into an argument with her over something petty like her touching something in his space or maybe he didn't like the lip gloss she wore this morning; that was his nature. The most insignificant things bothered him beyond belief.

Déjà just decided to ask her herself. She walked up to her and motioned for her attention. The janitor looked up at Déjà with a totally unconcerned look and continued to vacuum. Déjà then tapped her on her shoulder. Now the janitor seemed a little irritated with Déjà. She looked at Déjà and said extremely sarcastically, "Yes, how can I help you?"

Déjà responded "I'm sorry, but I'm in a very important meeting. I was wondering if you could vacuum later, possibly when we were done."

"No, I cannot," replied the janitor in a very unpleasant voice. "I'm very busy and I also have a very important meeting this afternoon, plus my worker didn't show up and I have to do his work. I'm the lead janitor; I give orders not take them."

The Video Call

Déjà was taken aback for a second. She thought to herself, *Does this bitch know who she is talking to: does she know the meeting she is having later is with me?* Déjà quickly calmed herself down and said, "So let me get this straight: you can't stop vacuuming for a little while and let us finish our meeting?"

The janitor looked at her up and down then switched the vacuum back on and vacuumed right around Déjà, as if Déjà was nothing. Déjà looked up to see her secretary witnessing the entire conversation. He said when Déjà got close to his desk, "No, no, I know you're not going to let that gorilla get away with that." He put his hands on his hips and stared at Déjà.

Déjà was furious. She said, "Don't worry; I will be talking to her later today."

He folded his arms, stomped his feet and shook his index finger back and forth slowly as he said, "No, no, Miss Thang, I need you to get her right now. Don't let that big wildebeest think she is getting away with being disrespectful to the junior executive of operations. Don't she know you run everything in this department?"

Déjà smiled and said, "If she don't, she sure is gon' learn."

After Déjà's meeting was over she had to interview some interns coming over from UCLA. They were a part of the young gifted scholars program Déjà's department ran. She met all the interns in the conference room. She wanted to see then before she picked her personal intern because last year she got stuck with a know–it-all smartass and she didn't have time this year to be bothered with that again. As she sized them up, she came across one particular candidate whose Christian Louboutin shoes caught her eyes. Déjà thought to herself, *Damn, she is almost as cute as me.* Déjà walked up to her and said, "Hello, my name is Déjà; what might yours be?"

The young lady stuck out her hand to shake Déjà's and said, "Hello, nice to meet you, Ms. Déjà. My name is Soni Lynn."

Déjà smiled and said, "First of all, what a pretty name, but please don't ever call me Ms. Déjà again. I'm only a few years older than you." They both started laughing. Déjà said, "Now tell me a little about you."

"Well," Soni Lynn said, "I graduated last year from UCLA with a BA degree in English with a minor in criminal justice. I'm currently attending UCLA School of Law."

Déjà could tell by the way Soni Lynn spoke she was extremely intelligent, with just the right amount of arrogance that made her likable.

"Good," Déjà replied, "now tell me something about your personal life: what do you like to do?"

Soni Lynn replied, "Well, I like to hang out with my friends and family. I have a twin brother and I like to go back home whenever possible."

Déjà liked this girl; she had a down-to-earth appeal to her, just the kind of intern Déjà wanted. She wasn't some snotty-nosed little spoiled rich kid who felt entitled. Déjà responded, "Home--where is home for you?"

Soni Lynn replied, "Harlem--I'm from New York."

The Video Call

After they chatted for a while Déjà handed out the interns' assignments, and she assigned Soni Lynn to work with her secretary. She jokingly told Soni Lynn, "Don't be scared of him because his bark is worse than his bite."

Then her secretary reminded Déjà of her meeting after lunch with the staff, including the janitorial staff. Also, he had taken it upon himself to gather up the complaints about the janitorial service.

Déjà spotted Luscious getting off the elevator; she forgot they had a lunch date. As the interns all walked out of the conference room Déjà introduced Soni Lynn to Luscious. As Soni Lynn said her hellos and goodbyes, Déjà's secretary and Luscious watched her walk away. Both of them could not help but notice her voluptuous shape. Déjà's secretary, being the smart mouth he was, said to Luscious while still watching Soni Lynn get on the elevator, "Um hum, now pick your face up off the floor because she is just as fabulous as you if not more, and you could tell that when she is fully dressed, unlike you!" then he looked Luscious up and down, rolled his eyes and let out a deep breath and said, "Did you do a mirror check, because if you don't know your ass and tits are dripping out everywhere. Oh yeah, did I mention Soni Lynn was much younger than you?"

Luscious just looked at him and gave him the evil eye. Déjà laughed at her secretary and told Luscious, "Never mind him; he hasn't had his daily dose of blood yet." They both started laughing and left for lunch.

As Déjà and Luscious were pulling out of the parking structure they noticed Soni Lynn getting in her brand new Range Rover sport hybrid. "Nice car," Déjà yelled out the window.

Soni Lynn smiled and said, "Thanks; it's a graduation gift from my granny."

"Nice granny," Déjà said.

"Best in the world," Soni Lynn said as she drove off.

At lunch Luscious pulled out her sketches of her new lingerie line. She said the name of it was "Thickies" and it was for full-figured women.

Déjà teased her and said, "I hope it's better than that two-piece bathing suit you had on in Mexico."

They both laughed and then Luscious said, "So how do you like your new intern this year, because last year you hated the one you had."

"Well, she seems cool; today was the first day I met her," Déjà replied.

"Well, let me know if you like her, because she would be perfect to model my new line of lingerie," said Luscious.

Déjà looked at Luscious and smacked her lips. She said, "What? You gon' let somebody model besides you? What the hell?" Déjà continued to say as she put the back of her hand on Luscious' forehead as if she was taking her temperature. "Are you feeling well? I can't believe you would let someone else model your lingerie."

Luscious laughed and said, "Girl, I'm getting old and if I want to sell my lingerie I'm going to need more than just my sexy ass. I'm going to need a squad of sexy bitches."

"Well, look at you, a little business woman. I guess you're going to finally put that degree you worked so hard for to use," replied Déjà. "It's about time." Déjà smiled but she didn't want to tell Luscious that she didn't think Soni Lynn would ever model her lingerie. Shit, Soni Lynn seemed to be bright and talented with a BA degree from UCLA and working on a Law degree. Plus, judging by the Range Rover Soni Lynn was driving, she already had money. Soni Lynn's arrogance was a clear sign to Déjà that modeling underwear was not going to be placed on her priority list. But Déjà figured she would at least mention it to Soni Lynn; that's the least she could do for Luscious. "So how's Blue eyes (the white boy they met at Luscious' apartment with his head between her legs before they went to Mexico)?" asked Déjà.

Luscious looked at Déjà like she had said something wrong. She said, "Girl, don't ever mention that fool again. That weirdo put a voice-activated tape recorder in my room and recorded all my private conversations, amongst other things."

Déjà looked at Luscious with her eyes wide open. "Bitch, please tell me he didn't record you having sex."

Luscious replied, "Girl, yes, and with other men; then he played it back to me. The little freak started crying, talking about how could I do this to him--what the fuck? He had to go."

Déjà started laughing; she looked at Luscious and said, "I told you about fucking with those white boys. They don't leave you; they kill you, bitch."

Then she started crying with laughter.

Luscious didn't find that to be funny; actually, she looked a little concerned and said, "Shit, I did a protection spell against his ass."

Déjà decided to change the entire conversation because she did not feel like hearing about Luscious' Voodoo religion. During their lunch Luscious mentioned that she might have a chance at choreographing a music video for one of her clients; she said during a lap dance he told her he was a producer and loved the way she danced. He asked if she would be interested in dancing in one of his videos he was working on. She said no but she would be interested in choreographing it. He said he liked her spunk. Luscious also informed the director that she knew a great hair stylist that could really do hair. Luscious said that he agreed to give both of them a try out if Luscious would agree to have dinner with him. Déjà smiled and thanked Luscious but told her that she had outgrown that dream years ago. Luscious asked her just to think about it.

Déjà said, "I hope this white boy ain't as crazy as Blue eyes," and started laughing.

Luscious replied, "Nope, and guess what? He's black."

"What, you finally coming back to the best side? Well, good for you; he must be one sexy motherfucker." Déjà agreed to think about it and told Luscious she had to get back to work because she had to put a janitor in her place.

On the way back to her office Déjà got a call from Mama Pearly asking her if she could please come down and take her to pay her bills. She said Chocolate was nowhere to be found and that all her nieces, nephews and trifling children were worthless. Déjà laughed and told her she would be there around 3:30, then Déjà asked her what happened to her paying her bills online? Mama Pearly said she forgot how, plus she liked to pay her bills the old fashioned way, with cash!

When she got back to the office Déjà was ready to get this lead janitor straight. The very thought of the janitor telling her how to run her department infuriated Déjà. *Who the fuck did she think she was? Hell,* Déjà thought. Shit, Déjà had gone to school earned both her degrees and was seriously thinking about going back to school to earn her PhD; she was gon' be damned if she let some janitor speak to her like she wasn't shit. Déjà let the rooms fill up with all the staff she supervised before she sat in her chair. She made sure she made a grand entrance so the lead janitor could know she fucked up. All through the meeting she kept watching the janitor squirm and toward the end she decided that she wasn't going to be rude and confront her in front of all the other supervisors. During the meeting she noticed that they were the only African Americans in the room. She didn't want to down another sister in a room full of white folks, even though she knew if the shoe was on the other foot that the janitor would.

After the meeting was over Déjà had her secretary summon the janitor to her office. Déjà's secretary seemed to get great pleasure from doing that; he even walked her right into Déjà's office, then he took a seat next to her with his iPad 2 to take notes. Déjà could see that even if she sent him to his desk he was just going to listen in on the conversation on the intercom; he was not going to be denied the pleasure of witnessing the janitor being put in her place. Déjà handed the janitor a copy of her job description and a copy of their company's policies and procedures, with the conduct code highlighted. Déjà gave her a few seconds to review it, then she reminded her of the incident they had earlier with the vacuum. The janitor tried to apologize but Déjà cut her off and handed her a list of complaints her secretary had gathered up from the other workers on that floor. Déjà said, "With a complaint list this long you should be fired. However, since I'm a reasonable and compassionate woman with concern for other people's feeling and their rights to be respected, unlike you, I'm going to give you one more chance. You will have a written warning in your record, and if I receive one more legitimate complaint you're out of here on your ass. Do I make myself clear?"

The janitor looked at Déjà and said, "Yes, but--"

Déjà stopped her. "There is no 'but'; your rude, disrespectful attitude and behavior are unacceptable. Please sign your written warning and clock out. You're dismissed for the rest of the day."

Déjà's secretary made coughing noises like something was stuck in his throat. Déjà looked over at him to see him cracking a half smile; she just shook her head at him and asked him to see the janitor out of her office. "With great pleasure," he replied.

Déjà sat back in her desk for awhile, then she remembered she had to go pick Mama Pearly up to pay her bills. After the long exhausting day Déjà had, she surely didn't feel like driving to Long Beach, but she promised Mama Pearly. As Déjà left her office she stopped to check on her new intern Soni Lynn. She spotted her at the desk her secretary had assigned to her. Soni Lynn was wiping off photos of her family and placing them on her desk.

"Nice looking family," Déjà said.

Soni Lynn smiled. She pointed at the picture. "That's my twin brother Xavier, my little brother Remy and my mommy--her name is Mary--and my stepfather Romello, and this whippa-snapper is my granny Suga Bell."

"Aw," replied Déjà, "your family looks like they're so much fun and your mom looks so young."

Soni Lynn smiled. "Oh my God, please don't ever tell her that."

Déjà cracked a smile. "Ok, if I ever meet her, I promise I won't say a word."

"Good," Soni Lynn said, "because you will probably get to meet them soon. My family is coming for a visit real soon and speaking of visits, I gotta get out of here. I promised my mommy I would check on her property down in Long Beach today. The tenants are complaining about gang bangers hanging out."

"Long Beach?" Déjà replied. "I'm on my way there right now; whereabouts in Long Beach are you going?"

Soni Lynn shrugged her shoulders and said, "Girl, I have no idea. I just Mapquested it and sent it to my navigation system. I have no idea where I'm going. I've never even been to Long Beach."

The Video Call

"I'm on my way to Long Beach right now," said Déjà, "and I sure don't feel like driving. Maybe if you drive I could show you where your mom's property is and then you could drop me to pay Mama Pearly's bills."

"Sounds like a deal to me," said Soni Lynn. On the way there they talked about their families and friends. Déjà explained to Soni Lynn how Mama Pearly was more of a mom to her than her own mom had been and that she and Chocolate were cousins. When they got there Mama Pearly insisted that they go meet her daughter's new boyfriend. She went on and on about how nice, polite, and handsome he was. She damn near said she thought he was too good for her daughter. They went to the back yard to meet him. Déjà couldn't believe her eyes when she looked up! *What the fuck?* she thought. *This can't be happening.* Chocolate's aunt's new boyfriend was Déjà's young lover Ghost who, if not for his age surely would have been her boyfriend (the fact that he didn't have a steady job Déjà didn't give a second thought),. Nobody really knew she was messing around with him, just Chocolate and Chagita, who truly didn't give a fuck; they thought he was a cute little boy. They even re-nicknamed him Pampers because they said it couldn't been that long since he had been out of them. Chocolate often teased Déjà that she was going to report her for child molestation, but Déjà said he may have been young in years but fully developed in mind, body, and skills. He was tall, medium build, extremely handsome, and hung like a horse. He had a pleasing personality, beautiful smile, and excellent manners. His grandmother had raised him well; he had that Southern charm that sucked Déjà right in--it was her weakness. His skills were developed way ahead of his years. Hell, just a glance at him had Déjà in a flashback and out of breath. She remembered all the times they'd been together; hell, she had just been with him a few weeks ago and he was on fire that night and his tongue had led her to a few cosmic orgasms. (While licking her he had given her options of which stroke he was going to use. He asked her which one she wanted: was it the slow, long round and round roll stroke of the tongue to her clitoris; was it the fast lick with the tip of his tongue to her clitoris; or was it the deep stroke of his tongue in and out of her vagina that was going to make her cum for him? Déjà opted for all three, and he obliged her with pleasure. After he had worked her up into a full blown tizzy with his tongue, he gave her hours of pleasure with his gigantic gift from God. He was like a windup toy with new batteries; he never got tired. The thing that drove Déjà crazy was that it was never about him. His sole goal was to please her, and he took great pride in his work. Déjà often thought she wanted to thank whoever the older lady was who trained him because she did a hell of a job. Afterwards he always held her and rubbed her down, told her how fucking sexy she was and that her body was a work of art that should be marveled. Déjà always complained that she was fat but he said he loved thick women; that all men wanted something to hold on to and that all her curves should be appreciated. He loved to watch her sleep naked. He said even her snoring was sexy.) Déjà snapped out of her daydream.

When he looked up to see her standing in front of him she could tell he was confused about her being there. Déjà just stuck out her hand and said, "Nice to meet you."

He looked over at Chocolate's aunt and said, "You know her?"

Déjà nodded her head yes. "Question is, how do you know her, but this is not the time or place." Then she walked away. He followed her out of the backyard into the house and tried to talk to her, but Déjà wasn't trying to hear what he was saying.

The Video Call

Soni Lynn caught them in the hallway. Déjà was on the verge of tears. Soni Lynn said, "Hey, what's going on? Is everything all right?"

Déjà looked up and with a tear rolling down her cheek, she said, "Yeah, everything is all right. My conversation with this nothing-ass nigga is over."

When she said that, he just looked at her and walked off. Déjà and Soni Lynn discussed the situation briefly. Déjà looked down at her phone to see several messages from him but neither did she read or respond to any of them. Besides, she and he had just had a discussion on how he was too young for her to even consider having a real relationship with. Shit, she was thirty-two, well-established, knew where she was going and what she wanted; she was career-driven and focused on the future. He was twenty-four, young, and a free-spirited idealist with big dreams. He was out trying to save the entire African American race from itself with his black power movement.

In the car while listening to Mama Pearly talk about how trifling her kids were, Soni Lynn texted Déjà the following quote: "We all know good dick comes with no job, no car, no license, five children three baby mamas, an E-class felony and a bad attitude." Then she added, "And in your case, fucking your cousin's auntie!!! Lol."

Déjà looked at Soni Lynn and said, "No texting while driving, please."

They both started cracking up laughing. Déjà didn't know what the hell she was going to do about that and at the moment she really didn't give a fuck! However she wished Chocolate would answer her phone, because she didn't want her telling her auntie about Ghost. As trifling as the auntie was, she had always been good to Déjà. Déjà didn't even try to understand where or how Chocolate's aunt knew him, but she did understand why she was with him. Damn, Déjà started to get pissed and jealous at the thought of him doing half the shit to Chocolate's aunt he did to her. She just shook her head and continued to agree with everything Mama Pearly said.

She was ranting and raving about how her no-good drug addict son was getting on her nerves and how her trifling daughter just dropped off her kids and left. Déjà and Soni Lynn just laughed. Déjà was accustomed to Mama Pearly's carrying on. Then she looked back at Déjà and said, "I don't know what's going on with you and that young man, but you need to know that men aren't toys to be played with when you feel like it; they have feelings, too. And from the way he looked at you, it seemed like he was in love with you. If you don't want him, stop playing house with him. Get my meaning?" Then she smiled at Déjà .

Déjà said, "Mama Pearly, how did you know?"

Mama Pearly smiled and said, "Baby, I know everything; besides I heard y'all in the hallway. And by the way, you pouting like you was five again is proof enough you got some type of feeling for that gorgeous baby and hell, I don't blame you; if I was younger I might give you a run for your money." Then she smiled and winked her eye at Déjà.

After they paid Mama Pearly's bills Déjà showed Soni Lynn her mom's property, which happened to be a few blocks away from Mama Pearly's house. The property was a huge condo complex a few blocks from the beach. It was a nice complex and appeared to be clean and well kept.

However there were a few undesirables hanging out front. Soni Lynn snapped pictures of them with her camera phone. She decided to let her mom handle that situation when she got to California in the coming months. Mama Pearly insisted that they stop at KFC to get her a two piece. On the way back to drop off Mama Pearly, she complained that she sure wished Déjà had picked her up in her two-seater convertible Porsche.

Déjà laughed and said, "Next time, Mama Pearly."

As they approached Mama Pearly's house they saw the ambulance and a large number of police officers. Mama Pearly started screaming, "Oh my Lord, please don't let it be the babies."

As they got out of the car they saw the stretcher coming out with Mama Pearly's youngest grandchild. Mama Pearly dropped to her knees in prayer while Déjà ran to the EMT to see what was going on. Déjà saw the police carrying a plastic Ziploc bag with a half of sandwich in it. "Officer, please tell me what happened here; this is my family."

He stopped and shook his head. He pointed to the little boy on the stretcher. "Is that your baby?"

"No," she replied, "it's my cousin's but she is not here; my granny is watching over him. Please tell me what happened."

He gave Déjà a look of disgust as he said, "This poor innocent baby ingested a controlled substance and somebody is in a world of trouble."

Mama Pearly was screaming when she heard that. "Lord no, not my baby, please say he is going to be all right."

The officer grabbed Mama Pearly, who was nearly fainting. He said, "Well ma'am, we don't exactly know what he swallowed; you see, whatever it was soaked into the sandwich he was eating. At least that's what we are assuming, since he was found unconscious and holding it in his hand. The teenage girl said her uncle was here dipping his marijuana stick in the clear liquid."

"What the hell?" Mama Pearly said.

The police officer explained that some drug addicts dipped their marijuana into what they called Sherm to get high. He explained that Sherm was really an animal tranquilizer called PCP and was very dangerous. He said he wasn't entirely sure about it but was willing to bet money that's what the child swallowed. He said most likely he sat his sandwich down and it soaked into the bread as if it was a sponge.

Déjà was just standing there in shock. Soni Lynn didn't know what to say. She said, "Is there anything I could do?"

Déjà asked the ambulance what hospital they were taking him to. Then she asked Soni Lynn to take them there. On the way to the hospital she tried several times to reach Chocolate, with no results. After hours, it seemed like, in the emergency room the little boy's mother showed up. Putting on a show for Déjà and Mama Pearly, she was screaming, "My baby, my baby."

Hell, Déjà thought, *your baby, bitch why did it take you hours to get here and why did you just drop them off in the first place?* By her appearance Déjà knew she was out getting high her damn self. It was so sad; Mama Pearly had eight children and all of them except one were on drugs or recovering from drugs. The one that wasn't on drugs moved to Denver with his white bitch wife and rarely even called Mama Pearly. Ever since he became a Sheriff he was too good for his family. Mama Pearly didn't give a damn anyhow; she said he got on her damn nerves anyway, acting like a little bitch.

Déjà stood up and said, "Where the hell you been? Your son is in there fighting for his life and you ain't nowhere to be found."

By this time Mama Pearly was trying to pick the little boy's mama up off the floor. She was putting on a show, rolling all over the floor, screaming and pounding on the ground. She looked like a fool, with snot running down her lips and her fake eyelashes coming off and that cheap wig hanging to one side. Mama Pearly was crying and trying to comfort her daughter. Déjà just stood there in disgust, looking at them.

The doctor finally came out and told them that the little boy was in critical condition and on life support. He told them he didn't think he was going to make it and if he did he surely was going to be brain damaged. Mama Pearly damn near fainted. Déjà looked over at his mother and the first words out of her mouth were, "Mama do you still have that insurance policy on him and am I still the beneficiary?"

That was it; Déjà hit the ceiling. She said, "Bitch, are you serious? Your fucking child is fighting for his life and yo' ho' ass is out here trying to come up on insurance money? Bitch, you ought to be ashamed of yourself.

The Video Call

You are a piece of shit; you sicken me."

Mama Pearly stepped between them and said, "Please don't argue." Then she gave Déjà that look that meant 'we will talk about it later.'

After Déjà calmed down she walked Mama Pearly down the hall to see her grandbaby. Mama Pearly couldn't stop crying and praying. As Mama Pearly sat by his side praying, Déjà heard police officers outside talking. They were discussing the child abuse case they were filing against whoever was responsible for the child at the time he ingested the controlled substance. An officer stopped at the door and said, "Mrs. Pearly Johnson, could you step outside please?"

Mama Pearly got up and walked to the hallway. The officer looked at the lead detective and he motioned his head yes. The officer told Mama Pearly she had the right to remain silent and began reading Mama Pearly her rights. Déjà couldn't believe it; she ran over to Mama Pearly's daughter. "Bitch, you gon' let them arrest yo' mama? You know damn well this is your fault." Déjà was so mad she got up in her face as if she was going to hit her.

The police warned her that if she didn't calm down she, too, was going to jail. Soni Lynn pulled Déjà; she told her to calm down, then she looked over at Mama Pearly and told her not to say a word. Déjà regained her composure and walked over to the officer. She said, "Could I please talk to my grandmother for a minute before you take her away?"

He agreed and then he said, "I know who is really responsible for this but unless she steps up there is nothing I can do."

The Video Call

Déjà walked over to Mama Pearly. She said, "Why would you go to jail for her?"

Mama Pearly calmly said, "Baby, I know you don't understand, but she is my baby; she already has two strikes and if she goes to jail for this, it will be her third. She will never come home. At the very least she will get ten years. I can't let my baby go to jail for ten years." She put her hand on Déjà's face and wiped her tears. "Besides, I'm an old lady no jury in the world would send me to jail. Don't cry; you will see. Now go call Chocolate and scrape me up some bail money, baby."

Déjà said, "Yes ma'am," then looked over at Mama Pearly's daughter and gave her a dirty look. She said, "Bitch, don't let me catch you on the street."

Soni Lynn advised Mama Pearly again not to say a word until her lawyer came. Then she got on the phone immediately with her Auntie Katy, who was a lawyer. As the police car drove off with Mama Pearly, Déjà called Chocolate again, with no answer. Soni Lynn tried to comfort Déjà but didn't want to cross the line. Déjà was her boss and Soni Lynn was sure she didn't want her seeing all this.

Chapter Five

Hot Mama

Déjà apologized to Soni Lynn for all the drama she had to witness today. Soni Lynn smiled and assured Déjà she had seen worse. They both shook their heads and laughed. Déjà said, "Girl I could write a number one best seller about all the ridiculous bullshit that happens in this family alone."

Soni Lynn laughed. "Girl, don't I understand!"

Déjà took off her four-inch platform heels and held them in her hand as she walked toward her car. "See you tomorrow, God willing," she screamed at Soni Lynn as she started up her car. As she drove away she noticed her gas light was warning her she only had 16 miles of fuel left. *Hell,* Déjà thought, *I can make it home. I will get some gas first thing in the morning.* As she was driving she thought about how pissed Chocolate was going to be when she heard about how her asinine auntie let her granny get arrested and refused to step up and take responsibility. Then it hit Déjà where Chocolate had disappeared to. She was on her conjugal visit with her husband and daughter. (Chocolate got married years ago to her childhood sweetheart Otis, who was also a Crip gang member/drug dealer. One day while cruising around down in Long Beach with Chocolate and their infant daughter, he spied a rival gang member he had a beef with riding along next to him. To avoid any incident, he sped up. He decided this wasn't the time or place for this altercation so he continued to drive on. However, the other gang member begged to differ. He pulled out his pistol, aimed it at the car and started shooting. Chocolate started screaming and using her body as a shield to cover the baby. Oddly, Otis didn't panic. He calmly told Chocolate to grab the wheel. Then he rolled his window down and started shooting back. Chocolate couldn't believe it; they were in a gun battle in broad daylight. The bullets were coming fast, the baby was screaming, and Otis was hit in the shoulder and slumping over the wheel. Chocolate grabbed the gun from his hands, aimed it at the driver and shot. One shot to the temple, and he was gone. She managed to pull the car over and she got the baby out. Otis told her not to say a word when the cops showed up. He took the rap for the murder. He told Chocolate he did it because he loved her and didn't want her to spend her life behind bars because of him. Plus, she had to raise the baby. Chocolate got time in juvenile hall because they had drugs in the car. While she was locked up, her daughter got diagnosed with autism. When she got released she married Otis in prison, with her grandmother's permission, because she was only seventeen.

She made the decision to send their daughter to this home for autistic children after she obsessively read everything about autism. The home taught the children how to take care of themselves and function in society. Chocolate's daughter was what they considered highly functioning autistic. She had a photographic memory and a considerably high IQ. However, she didn't like to be touched and had a rocking fetish.

Otis told Chocolate she didn't have to marry him, but Chocolate insisted. So he made a deal with her. She could have relationships with other men, as long as those other men understood their arrangement, which was monthly visits and conjugal whenever allowed.) Chocolate had been going on those conjugal visits for over 15 years and in that time she had never missed one. Like clockwork, she and the daughter were there. The daughter was now sixteen years old and talking about college. Chocolate always felt guilty because she thought it was her fault that the daughter was autistic because she had her when she was fifteen.

Déjà sure didn't want to tell her that Mama Pearly was in jail. Déjà was

praying the lawyer got her out before Chocolate returned. As she exited
the freeway she realized she had underestimated how far she really lived
from her job when she felt her car pulling from running out of gas. "Ain't
this a bitch," she screamed as she beat on the steering wheel with her
hands. "Fuck, this is all I fucking need," she continued to mumble as she
reached inside her glove compartment to get the number to her roadside
assistant insurance. Suddenly she realized she was on the exit and
blocking all traffic from exiting. *Oh my God,* she thought, *this is an
accident waiting to happen,* and in a panic from the thought of getting hit
by a car or even worse, her Jaguar being totaled by a semi-truck, she
called 911. The 911 operator dispatched a car to assist her. After the
officers moved her car off the off ramp, they insisted that she wait inside
her car for the roadside assistance to arrive. Déjà thanked them and
proceeded to make calls on her cell.

One of the cops stayed behind. When the other officer was out of sight he
approached Déjà and said, "If you don't mind, I'll wait with you. I
couldn't leave a beautiful lady like yourself out here alone. With all the
nut jobs running around ain't no telling what could happen." Then he gave
her the look all men gave her when they were checking her out.

Déjà had to admit she did feel safer with him out there with her. She
checked him out good. He was tall, thin, and dark. Clean-cut, he seemed
like a fairly decent man, plus he had a nice smile; that was a deal breaker
for Déjà--pretty teeth were a must! "Why thank you, officer. I'm sorry, I
didn't get your name."

He replied, "My name is Eric, and yours?"

Hot Mama

Déjà smiled and said, "Déjà."

"What a pretty name for such a pretty woman," he replied. "If you don't mind me asking, are you married?"

"No, I'm not," she responded, "and you, do you have a wife and kids?"

The expression on his face let her know the answer was yes. He proceeded to tell his story and what the hell, Déjà thought, she had time to listen; the damn tow truck said he was going to be at least forty-five minutes which really meant an hour and a half. He said he and his wife were divorced after six years and had two children whom they shared joint custody of. He told Déjà all about how he had his children every other weekend and all about the fun things they did together. He explained how the mom was already in a relationship with some loser neither he nor the children were fond of. Déjà liked how he seemed to light up when he spoke about his children. Déjà just listened and continued to ask all the right questions, and within twenty minutes of their conversation Déjà knew his entire life history. He told Déjà he became a cop because he witnessed his mom get killed by her girlfriend. He said his mom and her girlfriend got into a fight and the girlfriend, in a jealous rage, shot her then attempted to kill herself but failed and ended up blind and brain damaged. She received no jail time because the jury saw her condition and took pity on her. They gave her ten years' probation. Officer Eric seemed disappointed when the tow truck arrived. They had spent all that time talking and he forgot to ask for her number.

As the tow truck driver looked over the car, he looked at Déjà, then the officer. He said to Déjà, "Is that fool trying to holla at you? Déjà smiled, then the tow truck driver said, "Bastard should be out fighting crime, not trying to holla at stranded ladies."

Déjà laughed and said, "Knock it off."

After the tow truck driver filled her gas up, Déjà thanked Officer Eric for waiting with her and wished him good luck, then she drove off. She looked at him through her rearview mirror; she too was a little disappointed he didn't ask for her number. Déjà finally made it home. She was overjoyed to get out of those clothes and into a hot bath, then in her comfy bed. Her dog ran to her, then off to his kennel. *Damn,* Déjà thought, *he must be really tired.* As she ran her bath water she removed all her clothing, down to her panties and bra. She heard the phone ringing and thought that to be odd because no one ever called on the house phone. Something had to be wrong. She cringed at the thought of more drama. She picked up the phone. "Hello?"

The voice on the other end sounded so professional, she just knew something terrible had happened. "Déjà Blue Muhammad?"

Damn, Déjà thought, *that's my full government name; what the fuck is going on?* "Yes, this is she," she replied.

"This is Officer Eric. I was just calling to see if you made it home ok. I hope that's okay with you?"

After Déjà heard that she calmed down. She smiled and said, "I don't recall giving you my number, officer; however, thank you for checking. I'm good." Then she laughed.

He said, "I'm sorry but I ran your tags, then your name. I came up with your number and address. I couldn't let you get away without trying to get a date. I hope that's not too forward."

Déjà laughed and said, "Excuse me, Officer Eric, I think that's called invasion of privacy."

He replied, "Then what would you call sitting in front of your house?"

Déjà peeked out of the window to see his squad car parked in front of her house. She wasn't scared or frightened; she felt the chemistry between them when they were talking. She said, "I would call that stalking, which is against the law in fifty states; besides, how did you get past security? This is a gated community."

He laughed and said, "Remember, I'm the law."

Déjà was kind of turned on that he went through all the trouble of running her tags just to get her number. She decided to invite him in for coffee and donuts. She said, "Well, since you were so nice to me the least I could do is offer you coffee and donuts--don't all police like donuts?"

They both laughed. Déjà said, "Let me throw on something and I'll let you in." She put on an oversized red v-neck t-shirt and let him in.

He stood in the door for a second looking at Déjà. He said, "I'm sorry for staring, but I've never quite seen a woman looked that good in a t-shirt."

Before Déjà could respond she heard her dog barking and running up the steps. "Oh my God," Déjà said as she took off running. She forgot she had bathwater running. It had overflowed the entire bath room floor. "No-no-no," Déjà was shaking her head. "This is all I need."

Officer Eric calmly said, "You got a mop and towels?" He looked at how upset Déjà was and told her to have a seat and that he would clean up the mess. Déjà was so tired she just sat on the floor by the bed and watched him clean her bathroom. When he was done he placed the wet towels in the dirty clothes basket and reran her some bath water. After he emptied the wet towels in the washer, he turned on the washer, let the dog out the back door and put the mop up.

Déjà felt a little guilty for letting him get the water up all by himself. She said, "I'm so sorry. I don't even know you and you're cleaning up my house."

"Oh it's nothing, sweetie," he replied. "Now let's get you to the tub."

Déjà looked at him she said, "I guess you gonna bathe me, too; isn't that going above and beyond protecting and serving?"

He gently took her hands in his and led her to the tub. He had put bubble bath in the tub. Déjà didn't have the heart to tell him she didn't use bubble bath because it irritated her vagina. It was just there because it came with a gift set. Officer Eric told Déjà he would close his eyes while she undressed. He told her that the bubbles would cover her body when she got in the tub and he promised he wouldn't peek. Then he covered his eyes with his hands and said, "Tell me when."

Hot Mama

Déjà took off her clothes and stepped into the tub. The hot, sudsy water felt good. She sank down in the tub and closed her eyes. She sighed a sigh of relief. Then she said, "Open."

Officer Eric stood there and looked at her. He got two face towels off the towel rack. He knelt down beside the tub next to her. Gently he washed the makeup from her face. He grabbed a hair clip off the sink and clipped her hair up. He washed her neck, ever so softly massaging it. His hands were big and strong. Déjà relaxed her head in his hands. After he washed her face and neck he used the other towel for her body. He lathered up the towel. He started from her collar bone down to her breast; when he got there he stopped.

Déjà said, "It's okay; you can't see them."

He proceeded to wash first gently around one breast, then the nipple. Déjà saw him close his eyes as he slid the towel down her stomach to her thighs. Déjà placed one leg up on the tub. Then she guided his hand back up her thigh to between her legs. He stopped when he got there and looked at Déjà. He came in real close and said, "You are so beautiful," and then he began to wash her between her legs. He took long slow strokes. She could feel his entire hand cup her vagina. Slowly he kissed her, sucking her bottom lip and sliding his hands back up to her breast, massaging her nipples. Slowly Déjà stood up in the tub. He grabbed her, pulled her close to him, and as they stood there kissing, he rubbed every inch of her body. Déjà knew she was out of order for this behavior but hell, she had a terrible day. His touch was comforting, plus she was long overdue for a man's touch. As he kissed every part of her body she did absolutely nothing to stop him. He backed up and looked at her. He unstrapped his gun holster and laid it on the sink. As he unbuttoned his uniform shirt, Déjà watched with anticipation. Just like she had envisioned, he was perfectly toned and had the body of an African warrior. Damn, she couldn't wait to see what he was packing besides that gun. After he took off his shirt he grabbed a towel and dried Déjà off. He wrapped the towel around Déjà and pulled her close. She couldn't resist the temptation to kiss those chocolate muscles--first his neck, then his chest and stomach; then she stopped. Slowly she unzipped the pants. And just like she suspected, the gun wasn't the only big thing he was packing, and it was loaded and ready to blow. Déjà pulled it out so she could get a good look at it. *Yes,* she thought, *he is circumcised.* An uncircumcised dick was another deal breaker for her. They made their way to the bed. Déjà had to admit that Officer Eric's foreplay was exhilarating. By all means she was hot as fish grease and wet and ready. Then out of nowhere she heard a voice.

"Chief, we have a situation."

Déjà jumped up, a little frightened.

Officer Eric took a deep breath and said, "Sorry gorgeous, that's my walkie-talkie; gotta answer that." He walked to the bathroom and began to speak. He walked back in the room he said, "Sorry, I got a situation that requires my attention, and yes, it's an emergency, because only an emergency could make me walk away from all this."

"Did I hear them refer to you as Chief?" Déjà asked.

"Yeah," he responded, then he pointed to his uniform. Déjà had never even noticed his gold badge clearly said chief.

Déjà looked him up and down and said, "You kind of young to be the chief."

He smiled as he buttoned up his clothes. He said, "Nope, just look young, love; I assure you I feel every day of my age."

"And that age is what?" Déjà asked. (She wasn't really concerned with his age. Age had never mattered to Déjà; hell, she was dating Ghost and he was eight years younger than her and now that she thought about it, she was still pissed with him.)

He looked at her and said, "We are all over 21, and that's really all that matters."

Déjà agreed and then she said, "Well, be safe, Chief."

He held her hand. "If I did anything tonight that offended you, I'm truly sorry; it's just that I couldn't help myself. Let me make it up to you. Dinner anywhere you like the next time I'm down here?"

"Down here?" Déjà replied. "Where are you from?"

He told her he was from up north, near the Oakland area, and that he was down here observing the LAPD for some possible tips on how to train his narcotic squad. He said he just happened to be on his way back to his hotel when he heard that 911 call she made, and since she was blocking his exit he decided to stop and help. Lucky him, he said. He said his plane was leaving at 6:00 pm later that day. He said he was only sorry he met her his last day here. He said he had been here three days observing LAPD, and he wasn't impressed.

Déjà laughed and said she didn't think anybody was impressed with the LAPD. Then Déjà thought she'd ask about Mama Pearly's case. What the hell; he wasn't chief of Long Beach Police but maybe he could pull some strings and get something done. Déjà thought twice about asking him; she didn't want him to think she was ghetto, but what the hell, she thought "A closed
 mouth don't get fed" is what Mama Pearly always said. She told him all about what had happened.

Surprisingly, he wasn't shocked. He told her that the commissioner of Long Beach was an old friend of his and that he would see what he could do. "But don't count on it, because the law is the law."

Déjà put her cell phone number in his and kissed him goodbye. Damn, she was tired. She thought all the drama going on was unreal. Chagita was out of control, Chocolate was MIA, the drama at work with the janitor, Mama Pearly getting arrested, the baby on life support, Chocolate's aunt fucking her young lover, and to top all that off, she was just about to have sex with a man she didn't know from Adam! *What the fuck?* she thought. Then she looked over at her night stand to see the invitation to her parents thirty-fifth anniversary party, which was rapidly approaching, and she totally didn't want to go to. She couldn't even believe her dad had been married to her mom for that long. Her mom was beyond a bitch. She flipped the invitation over so she didn't have to look at it. She glanced over at the clock. *Damn,* she thought, *it's three am.*

As soon as her head hit the pillow, she was out. The alarm clock went off at six-thirty sharp. Déjà got up, walked to the bathroom and looked at the tub. She couldn't help but smile when she recalled what had just happened a few hours ago. She checked her cell and smiled. She had a text message from Chief Eric: "Hope you have a beautiful day, beautiful... Chief."

Déjà showered and dressed, then she called her secretary to get her schedule. He assured her she had no pressing business to handle today. However, she decided to go in anyway and leave early to go see about Mama Pearly. She tried Chocolate again and she still wasn't answering. Déjà spent a few hours at work issuing orders. She spoke with Soni Lynn and apologized again for last night. Soni Lynn gave her some helpful advice on how to handle Mama Pearly's case and a number to a good lawyer.

Déjà told Soni Lynn she appreciated the number; however, her family already had the best criminal defense lawyer in the area. Déjà left early that day and when she got to Long Beach later that afternoon, to her surprise, Mama Pearly was sitting on the couch praying. "Hey lady," Déjà said, smiling and hugging Mama Pearly. "Who busted you out?"

Mama Pearly said, "Child, I don't know who did what; all I know is some officer came and got me. He said I had to appear in court on this date." Then she handed Déjà a paper with a court date schedule three months later. "Then he released me," she continued. "I caught a cab home and now I'm here, praise the Lord."

Déjà said, "How is the baby doing?"

Mama Pearly said, "Praise God, he woke up this morning asking for pancakes. They're doing some tests. The doctor said he got a long road ahead of him."

Papa Johnson (Mama Pearly's husband) walked in, all dressed up in his Sunday best and said, "Hey Chunky" (Déjà's nickname from when she was little).

"Hey Papa Johnson, where you going all dressed up?"

He said, "Well, down here to the hospital to sit with the little one. See you later, Chunky." Papa Johnson and Mama Pearly had been married for so many years they lost count. They had eight children together and a countless number of grandchildren. Papa Johnson was a retired longshoreman.

As he drove off Déjà smelled something delicious cooking in the kitchen. She got up to investigate that delicious smell. She saw Mama Pearly's trifling daughter standing there making plates. Déjà just turned and walked away. Mama Pearly said, "Don't be mad at her; she is just in a bad way right now, and who can she turn to if not her family?"

Déjà knew Mama Pearly was right so she agreed not to argue with her. She hollered from the kitchen, "Chunky, you hungry? I made smothered pork chops, greens and cabbage, fried corn, yams and corn bread."

Damn, Déjà thought, *that sounds fucking delicious.*

Mama Pearly looked at Déjà and winked her eye. She said, "That's her way of saying she is sorry."

Hot Mama

As she sat the plates down in front of them, she looked at Déjà and said, with tears in her eyes, "I'm going to rehab. I'm going to get better, I promise."

Déjà didn't say a word; she just picked up her plate and started eating. *Damn, this food is good,* Déjà thought; if Mama Pearly's children couldn't do anything else, those bitches could throw down in the kitchen. Déjà kept checking her phone; to her surprise, she was eagerly awaiting a call or text from Chief Eric but he hadn't texted since this morning. Déjà wasn't going to dare call him; she was just going to wait. As they finished up their food, Déjà checked her emails and called to check in with her secretary. He said all was well at the office so she could stop calling. She got a call from Chocolate saying to meet her at her apartment on top of her tattoo shop. Chocolate sounded a little down already Déjà decided to wait and tell her about all the drama with Mama Pearly.

Déjà kissed Mama Pearly goodbye and walked to her car. As she hit the alarm she saw Mama Pearly's daughter approaching her. "You think you could loan me a few bucks to get a pack of cigarettes?" she asked Déjà.

Déjà just shook her head and reached down in her purse. Then Déjà said, "When you going to the hospital?"

Her response floored Déja. "Papa Johnson is going to sit with him today while I handle some business."

Déjà just looked at her and said, "Bitch, you are ridiculous," and drove away. Déjà called Luscious to fill her in on what was going on. Before she got to Chocolate's she stopped to get a bottle of wine. She knew she was going to need a drink after she told Chocolate what had gone down. She used her key to let herself in Chocolate's apartment. Chocolate had all the lights out and was in the bed with all the covers over her head. Déjà could hear her crying as she walked toward her.

"Sweetie, what's wrong?" Déjà just assumed she was crying because she missed Otis and her daughter. She saw Chocolate had pulled out all the family photo albums, but for some reason she had stabbed all Otis' pictures. Then Déjà assumed they got into one of their many disagreements. Whatever it was this time must have truly pissed Chocolate off. Chocolate pulled the covers back. Oh my God. Déjà took a deep breath when she saw Chocolate's face. Her eyes were swollen shut from crying. Déjà was shocked; she had never seen Chocolate quite so upset, not even at her mother's funeral. Chocolate was the type to keep her emotions to herself, unlike Déjà, who was emotionally dysfunctional at times.

"Tell me what happened, sweetie," Déjà said to Chocolate as she hugged her. At that point Chocolate collapsed in Déjà's arms. She was trying to talk but couldn't form a sentence for crying so hard. Déjà made her some tea and toast. She sat it in front of Chocolate, then she said softly, "Now tell me all about it."

Chocolate reached over in her dresser drawer and pulled out a bottle of Jack Daniels and poured it in her tea. Déjà thought, *Let me get comfortable, because if this bitch had to pour Jack Daniels in her tea just to tell me what happened I know it's going to be mind blowing.*

Chocolate started off by telling her how she went to the prison for her

conjugal visit. She said she knew something was wrong when the
correctional officers started acting nervous when they saw her. She said it
took forever to get checked in and normally she went straight to the back.
This time they asked her to have a seat because the sergeant wanted to talk
to her. She said she just figured Otis had gotten into some trouble for
having that cell phone he called her on once a day. When all the visitors
went to the back, they called Chocolate to the office on the side. She said
that's where the sergeant informed her that Otis refused to have his
conjugal visit. As a matter of fact, he asked that she be dropped from his
visiting list. Chocolate said she was in shock. She said she was confused;
she didn't know what to say. She asked the officer why he would say that.
The sergeant said he didn't know and didn't particularly care. However,
she had to leave the prison grounds immediately. They handed her
belongings and bid her a good day. Chocolate said she stood outside in the
prison parking lot trying to get her thoughts together. After a few minutes
she saw a correctional officer walking toward her car.

She said she walked over to her and said, "I'm going to tell you something
woman to woman, just because if I was you I would want to know; the
truth is, sisters gotta stick together."

Chocolate looked her up and down; she said she really didn't care for that
bitch because Otis had already told her she tried to throw him some pussy
on a few occasions but he refused her. He said she wasn't his type.
Chocolate said she listened because she wanted to get to the bottom of the
situation. The correctional officer looked down at the ground she said, "I
really don't know how to tell you this but Otis refused his visit because his
cellmate, who is apparently his boyfriend now, said if he went to his visit
he was going to kill himself. He told Otis that he was tired of being his

secret and from now on it was going to be just them two, not y'all three."

Déjà's mouth dropped wide open and her eyes bulged out. "Bitch, what the fuck you said?" came out of Déjà's mouth. "You trying to tell me Otis is fucking his cellmate? Get the fuck out of here. I don't fucking believe it." Déjà was going on and on about the situation. She could tell it was upsetting Chocolate more. Déjà calmed down; she looked at Chocolate and said slowly, "Ok, then what else happened?"

Chocolate said she didn't believe her but the officer said she was dead serious and it had been going on for a while. But all the other inmates were too scared of Otis to say anything. She advised Chocolate to just wait for her Dear John letter. Chocolate said she could have sworn that raggedy bitch smirked as she said it. Chocolate said she could tell she was getting pleasure out of crushing her feelings. Chocolate said she just drove off and called the cell phone Otis had. She said that some other inmate answered and told her that he don't know what happened, but earlier that day Otis' cellmate tried to hang himself and Otis went crazy and tore up the whole cell. He said it took five guards and a blast from the stun gun to hold him down, then they dragged him out. He said nobody had any idea where they took him. He said that the cellmate was in the county hospital under suicide watch and their block was on lock down until further notice. Then Chocolate rambled on and on about her daughter O'shay and about how they weren't good enough to be her parents.

Déjà comforted Chocolate the best she could, then she told her the drama, which sent Chocolate into overdrive. She was running around the house looking for her guns. Déjà managed to convince her not to go looking for her aunt tonight. Instead, they drove to the hospital to see the baby. He was doing good; he seemed like he was still a little high, but for the most part he was talking and acting normal despite what the doctors were saying. They said he was going to have brain damage and a list of various other problems. However, it didn't seem like it.

Chocolate and Déjà left the hospital, and as they drove home Déjà told Chocolate all
 about Chief Eric. Chocolate was laughing. She said, "Bitch, you too much--you just randomly fucking officers?"

They both cracked up laughing, then Déjà got the call she was waiting on. "Hey," Déjà said when she answered the phone

"Hey yourself, how was your day?" he replied. He and Déjà talked for a while, and he informed Déjà that he got held up in Los Angeles traffic and missed his flight. He said he got rebooked to an early morning flight and would love to have dinner with her tonight at his hotel suite. He told Déjà he was staying at the "W" next to the Staple center in Los Angles. Déjà agreed to meet him there in the restaurant downstairs. She showered and changed at Chocolate's house and pulled together a cute outfit from Chocolate's closet, which was almost impossible given Chocolate's outrageous style. Luckily, she already had on some fabulous silver wedges. In Chocolate's closet she found a beautiful coral colored wrap-around blouse and nice jeans that fortunately Chocolate hadn't cut up yet. She took her time to make sure her makeup was on point.

"Damn, you going all out for the Chief; he must have that magic touch," Chocolate teased Déjà as she got dressed. When Déjà was walking out the door Chocolate yelled, "Keep your panties on, bitch."

Déjà smiled to herself as she thought, *Sure I'll keep them on; he can just pull them to the side.*

The Chief was waiting for her in the lobby. Déjà couldn't help but notice that the Chief cleaned up very well. He had on a tan suit and cream colored dress shirt. He got up to greet Déjà with a hug and kiss to the cheek. His scent was intoxicating. They chatted for a while in the lobby then sat in the restaurant for what seemed like hours just talking. Déjà liked him; he was down to earth, easygoing and they had a lot of things in common. Déjà liked the fact that he had real conversation; he wasn't just baiting her for sex. He was genuinely interested in what she had to say. He showed her pictures of his two young children, ages seven and eight. After dinner they had drinks at the bar and talked some more.

Déjà looked at her phone. Time had been slipping away; it was 1:30 am. Déjà said her goodnights as he walked her to her car. They hugged and kissed. Déjà felt the strong chemistry they had again. He held her tightly and whispered in her ear, "I don't want to let you go; stay with me. We won't do anything you're not comfortable with, I promise."

Déjà bit her bottom lip and said, "That's the problem: I'm too comfortable with you, and I can't deny that I want you. The problem is not what you might do to me, it's what I might do to you."

He smiled at that and led her up the elevator to his suite. "Man, it must be awfully good being the Chief," Déjà said as she looked around his suite.

"It has its perks," he responded, "but for the most part, it's hectic and stressful."

Hot Mama

Déjà could tell by the way he talked he really enjoyed his job and was good at it. He said he joined the police department after he did six years in the Coast Guard. They continued to talk for awhile. He turned the radio on to some jazz music which, combined with the wine Déjà was drinking, put her into a relaxed, mellow mood. Their chemistry was amazing; although she had only known him for a day, it felt like she had known him for years. She fought with herself as long as she could not to touch him. All it took was one touch; their hands touched as he refilled her drink, and that was it. His touch was soft and gentle, with just the right amount of force. As he slid her black lace panties down, she remembered what Chocolate had said to her right before she left: "Bitch, keep your panties on." She smiled to herself. It was surely too late, for that one touch and those panties were coming off. She felt his lips and tongue on her stomach, and down and down they went until he had her ass cupped in his hands and his tongue on her spot.

Déjà thought, *Damn, that bitch Chocolate must be psychic, because he has the magic touch and a magic tongue.* God damn, the Chief had some skills. Déjà had been around the block a few times. His skills were only comparable to one and that was Ghost, but in this moment he was the farthest thought from her mind. The things the Chief whispered in her ear sent chills down her spine, and he backed up everything he said, too. The Chief was giving Déjà a run for her money; she had to reach deep into her bag of tricks. But she didn't mind; for some reason she couldn't understand, she wanted to please him and from the way he was biting his bottom lip trying not to moan and that tight grip he had on her hips as she rode his thick ten inches, she could tell he was pleased. As she fell asleep in his arms, she wondered what the hell had she gotten herself into.

96

Chapter Six

Dog Killer

Dog Killer

The next morning Déjà awoke to strong hands rubbing her lower back and a sexy voice saying, "Good morning beautiful". That voice was seductive. He pulled her in close to him and somehow she ended up under him once again. She was a little sore from last night but still she wanted more of him; he was amazing. In the middle of the workout he was giving her, her phone rang. Needless to say, it was going to have to wait; besides, she was too busy screaming in the pillow and holding on the bed post from the pounding he was giving her. Déjà fell back to sleep afterward.

This time when she awakened she saw a vase of wild flowers on the table and a plate of what looked like breakfast. Déjà called for the Chief but as she sat at the table she saw a note next to the wildflowers that read, "Sorry beautiful, didn't want to wake you. You were sleeping so peacefully. I had to catch my flight. I left four tickets to the championship game at the Stable Center. Hope you enjoy. Until next time, Eric."

As Déjà sat there eating scrambled eggs and toast she was trying to figure out what to think about this note. Should she be upset or not? The note was a little impersonal after the oh-so-personal time they had just shared. Déjà picked her phone up to check her email and noticed all the texts from Luscious begging her to go to some video shoot and do some model's hair. Déjà thought she had already informed Luscious that she'd given up that dream years ago. She also had text messages from Ghost, who at this point she really didn't want to talk to. It didn't matter that she had just spent the night with the chief; Ghost was still at the very top of her fuck-you list. And speaking of hair, hers was a mess. Luckily this fancy hotel room came with a flat iron. There was a knock on the door. Déjà didn't know rather to answer it or not, then she heard a voice. "Ms. Déjà Muhammad?"

Damn, is everybody using my full government name? she thought. When she opened the door she saw a man in a white hotel uniform and a massage table. He said, "There was a deep tissue massage ordered for you this morning by a Chief Eric."

Déjà looked at the worker as she tapped her bottom teeth with her short French tipped nail. She said, "And is this deep tissue massage paid for?"

He looked confused, then he looked down at his order form and replied, "Well, it seems like it is, and it also seems like you have an open account to order whatever you like, so where would you like me to set up?"

"Do you mind if I shower first?" she asked the worker.

He looked at her with a slight grin and said, "Long night?" He agreed to come back in one hour. When she asked him what time check-out was he informed her that this suite was leased out by some government agency; therefore there was no check out time. Since it was Saturday she had no place to be in particular so she moseyed around the suite. She showered, flat ironed her hair and called Luscious to bring her some clean clothes and underwear. Chocolate was her first choice but she was still pining away from Otis and O'Shay, as she always did for a few days after her visit. Déjà knew Luscious was going to continue to try to pressure her to do the hair for the video shoot. Déjà looked in the mirror and thought, *Hell I'm excellent at it,* as she fixed her clip-on pieces. She swooped her bangs over her left eye for that sexy look. She pointed in the mirror at herself and said, "Bitch, you know you dead wrong for this bullshit here! You are fucking the Chief of Police that you don't even know, you in some hotel room, and to top all that off bitch, you enjoying it! You a hot mess!" Then she laughed.

As she was getting her deep tissue massage Luscious showed up. The outfit she had on was beyond words. Too short, too tight, all wrong and not to mention the honey blonde wig all the way down her back; however, her shoes were the bomb. Déjà was sure the massage therapist thought they were whores. Déjà told Luscious all about her night and the Chief. The massage therapist was so intrigued in Déjà and Luscious' conversation he also gave Luscious a massage. As he was packing up his stuff to leave he gave both ladies a business card. He left and they continued to gossip about Chief Eric. They heard a knock on the door. Déjà answered the door. She saw a lady cop standing there. "Yes, may I help you?" Déjà asked her.

The lady cop looked a little puzzled. She said, "I'm sorry, I was looking for Eric," and by the dirty look she gave Déjà, she knew she was more than just a fellow officer.

Déjà replied, "Well, he isn't here at the moment and I'm really not sure when he's going to return."

The lady cop seemed a little disappointed. She said, "I'm sure you're not; however, the other night I lost my earring here. Do you mind if I come in to look in the bedroom for it?"

Déjà was trying to be polite but this bitch was being rude and she had a stank attitude. So Déjà decided to give her a taste of her own medicine. Déjà replied, "I'm afraid not. Unless you have a warrant you're going to have to search for your earring at a later date, but I'm sure they weren't that expensive so replacing them shouldn't be a problem, plus I was all over the bed last night and this morning and I didn't see it." Déjà could tell she was pissed.

She said, "If you could just tell him I came by, I would appreciate it," then she put her hand up and said, "Never mind, I'll just call him."

At that very moment Déjà's phone rang. She looked down; it was none other than Chief Eric. Déjà told the lady cop, "Hold on, this is him calling now."

She was furious and stormed away from the door to the elevators. Luscious was in the background pointing to the phone and barking like a dog. Luscious said, "I think Chief Eric might be a playa" and fell on the sofa laughing. Déjà covered the phone so he couldn't hear. Déjà thanked the Chief for the beautiful wildflowers, breakfast and massage, as well as the tickets to the championship game. Then she told him all about his lady cop friend. He apologized for that, but Déjà told him he didn't owe her an apology because she didn't even know him two nights ago. Their conversation was nice, and Déjà enjoyed talking to him. She was kind of wishing he was still in LA so she could see him. After they hung up Déjà realized she was missing him, but how could that be? She didn't even know him. Déjà got dressed and she and Luscious left.

Luscious had finally convinced Déjà to come to this video shoot she was choreographing. Déjà could tell Luscious was excited about it. They left the hotel. Déjà drove Luscious to her car. As they approached Luscious' car they saw somebody was sitting on the hood. As they got closer they saw it was Blue Eyes (the white boy with his head between Luscious' legs). Before Luscious got out of the car she reached down in her bag and got her Mace. She seemed to be a little frightened, so Déjà popped the trunk and grabbed her Louisville slugger. Déjà asked Luscious what the hell was going on with this dude. Luscious said he was following her and calling, begging her to be with him.

He got down off the hood and said, "Is this what you do now? You sneak off early in the morning and meet your boyfriends in expensive hotel rooms? What about me? I called you all day and you refuse to answer my calls."

Luscious responded, "Didn't I tell you to leave me alone and stop following me? I'm going to call the cops."

He just stood there shaking his head and rumbling on about how Luscious used him and played mind games with him. He was pitiful. Déjà had heard enough; she shook her bat at him and said, "Stay the fuck away from her or you gon' get yo' head busted open."

He couldn't believe it; he ran to his car and drove off. Déjà was extremely concerned after Blue Eyes drove away. Luscious was still looking a little frightened. Déjà reassured her that he wasn't crazy enough to do anything to her, although she did have her doubts. After she called to check on Chocolate she and Luscious made their way to the Staple Center for the playoff games. Even though Déjà wasn't a big basketball fan, seeing all those people so excited over a basketball game did pique her interest.

Valet parking came with those complimentary sky box tickets the Chief had given her. "Sweet ride," said the valet as she took the keys to Déjà's

Porsche. "I just might take that for a spin while you guys watch the game," said the valet.

Déjà smiled and looked at the young girl. She said "Girl, just make sure you don't kill nobody and have it back before the game is over."

The young girl said, "Hey now" and gave a snap, and they both started laughing.

The sky box was the same as any other skybox Déjà had been to. Mister was a retired NBA player so he took her to games quite often, although she didn't understand why. Hell, all he did was complain about the NBA still owing him money and defaulting on his contract. Déjà knew it was just bitter talk because they both knew he couldn't play with an injury as serious as his. He also lost all his endorsements, which really hurt his ego and his pockets. But he was smart; he took all his money and started a promotions company and he was doing really well.

Déjà and Luscious settled in to watch the game finally, after Luscious complained about the liquor selection and insisted they restock it with Ciroc and cranberry juice. What the fuck? Déjà thought. *This bitch is tripping. Her normal drank is wine and today, after Blue Eyes scared the shit out of her, it's all of a sudden Ciroc and cranberry juice.*

Déjà was enjoying the game but Luscious looked a little on edge and her phone was blowing up with texts. Déjà assumed they were from Blue Eyes and for every text she received, she took a shot of Ciroc straight; fuck the cranberry juice. She got so wasted she fell asleep by halftime. So Déjà just sparked up a conversation with the man sitting next to her. By the end of half time she knew his entire life history.

At halftime Déjà thought she saw Soni Lynn on the floor talking to one of the players. At a closer glance she was sure it was Soni Lynn. Soni Lynn was in an intense conversation with one of the star basketball players and to top that off, the little heffa was sitting on the floor. Damn Déjà thought, floor seats. Shit, Déjà would rather be down there than way up top in that fucking sky box. But the real question in Déjà's head was where the hell did Soni Lynn get floor tickets and why was she talking to that particular player? Was that her dude? "Go Soni Lynn," Déjà said out loud.

When the game was over Déjà sat around until all the people had left the skybox, then she woke Luscious up. "Bitch, wake yo' drunk ass up; we gotta go," Déjà said as she shook Luscious.

Waking up and looking around like she didn't know where she was, Luscious said, "Bitch, why you let me drink that much?"

Déjà laughed and said "I didn't let you do nothing; that was all you."

They made their way to the escalator with Déjà trying to hold Luscious' big ass up. On the ride home Déja got a call from Mister. "Hey sexy lady," she heard. Those words normally sent butterflies to her stomach but oddly this time they didn't.

Déjà replied, "Didn't I tell you I don't date married men? I'm not trying to be mean, but you have to stop calling me."

After Déjà hung the phone up Luscious (who was supposedly sleep) came out of her coma and said with her best country accent imitation, "Why Déjà Blue Muhammad, I do declare I thinks you in love with this chief. Damn, he got you turning down the love of your life. Shit, I got to meet this fool. Hell, he got a brother?"

Déjà turned her nose up at Luscious and said, "Damn Robin Marie Bennett, you had to use my entire government name," and they both fell out laughing.

Then Déjà turned the conversation back on Luscious. She warned her again to be careful of Blue Eyes and then she went further to get all in her business about this producer Luscious seemed to be so taken with. During their conversation Déjà's phone rang again. It was Mister. She knew he was going to call back again. She was just going to have to block his number; she had made her mind up she was done with him. Even though she was distracted by the chief, she was still pissed with her young lover Ghost. She listened to all Ghost's messages. She was going to let him sweat it out a few more days before she called his ass back .. That was, until she got home and stalked Ghost's social network page and saw his status. She called him and cursed him out something terrible. After the huge blow-up, knock-down–drag-out fight of words they had, Déjà lay in the middle of her bed in complete darkness crying uncontrollably and brokenhearted over the completely irrational, dysfunctional, and complex relationship they continued to pursue. Neither one of them would let go and just walk away. Either she wasn't speaking to him or he wasn't speaking to her. She was already in a sort of relationship with The Chief, and he was in and out of several, including one with Chocolate's aunt. Ghost often pressured her to end her relationships to be with him, which wouldn't have been an issue if he was stable and had his shit together

Dog Killer

(despite the fact he was younger than her). He was in the habit of roaming from woman to woman looking for Miss Right, and she was comfortable hanging out with the chief. However, they both shared an unhealthy attraction to one another that seemed never-ending. No matter how long they stayed apart, somehow they always made their way back to one another. They seemed to have an unbreakable bond and mutual physical attraction to one another. Today was just one episode of many. Déjà was all fired up over that social network post he had posted. Even though he had already de-friended her from his page after she cut up at Mama Pearly's house, he had an open page and knew she looked at it daily. The post read something to the effect that he was in a relationship with some desperate, low self-esteem, unsure of herself heffa whom she knew had pressured him to post it just to reassure her he was really interested in her. Her issue wasn't that he posted it; it was that he didn't forewarn her about it.

She didn't care about that; she knew he didn't love that woman. She just wanted him to finally stand up and be the man she knew he was: strong, intelligent, kindhearted, and loving. He just needed to be independent, and it seemed like he was scared to be out on his own, void of any influence from some woman. She always told him he had an Oedipus complex and his fetish for older women proved it. She looked at her phone and reread the text she'd sent him and analyzed the ones he sent her. He was pissed with her today but not so pissed he would send a text that sent her over the deep end. However, after she sent the text that said, "You ain't shit, if you died that day I wouldn't cry and I hope something bad happens to you," he called her and blasted her out good. He said she only wanted him for sex and to be her side nigga and he was tired of her playing games. He said if she couldn't make a choice then he was going to choose for her. He told

107

her to lose his number and not ever text, call, or send him any more pictures (he loved sexy pictures of her). After he blasted her out and hung up in her face, she threw her phone across the room. It crashed into the wall and cracked the entire front screen, but she didn't give a damn at that point.

A few seconds later she heard it ringing. She got up and ran to get it, hoping it was him calling to apologize, but it wasn't him. It was The Chief. She calmed herself down to answer the call. He said he just called to say goodnight and asked her what she ate for dinner. She just lied and told him she ate a sandwich. Hell, as furious as she was she didn't have an appetite. She soon found it difficult to breathe or sleep. She couldn't believe that this one man who wasn't even hers had this much control over her emotions. How could it t be that he could send her into a outright meltdown over something as petty as a social network post? She often told herself she was going to get therapy for her outrageous behavior that she always rationalized in her mind as okay. She convinced herself that she knew she was crazy and as long as she owned up to her bullshit and saw everything for what it really was and didn't lie about it, then in her mind it was all good. She knew she was selfish, arrogant, self-centered and outright ridiculous, but so what?

After a few days Luscious had convinced her to go to this producer's house to do these video girls' hair. When they got there it was just like she imagined: video whores everywhere running around half naked and rappers smoking weed and drinking. To Déjà's surprise Luscious was on top of her game business-wise. She was on point; however, her outfit was too sexy, as usual, bordering on offensive. Luscious was all business that day. She had her sketches, her concept was on point and she worked the hell out of those dancers. Déjà styled all the girls' hair to Luscious' concept. Then Luscious introduced Déjà to Mr. Producer. He appeared to be an ok gentlemen; he didn't seem shady or too over the top, unlike Luscious' usual selection of gentlemen friends. His personal chef made them lunch and they had a nice conversation. Luscious seemed to be taken with this man. Déjà was puzzled because normally if they weren't white, Luscious didn't give them a second look.

As the producer worked Luscious and Déjà, being the nosey heffas they were, took a personal tour of his home. *Damn, this fool is filthy rich,* Déjà was thinking. But she knew it didn't matter to Luscious because money was not a factor in her relationships. She was one of those free spirits and based her relationships on soul connection, chemistry and all that type of bullshit. She was the type of person if she found out you were born at the wrong time of the day and y'all's stars didn't align you were out.

They found themselves upstairs in the west wing, probably somewhere they shouldn't have been. Déjà heard talking coming from one of the rooms as they passed. The door was open so Déjà peeked inside. She saw an old lady sitting in the chair watching TV and oddly having an entire conversation with it. As they walked off she said, "It's rude to spy on people, little whores."

Déjà and Luscious walked back to the room. "Excuse me," Luscious replied, "are you talking to us?"

"Well, you two are the only ones sneaking around my son's house peeking in the doors, so yeah, I guess so. For the record, he normally doesn't bring his whores to the west wing, so that lets me know either you two are lost or being nosey!" Déjà put her hand over her mouth and turned to laugh. The old lady said, "Come in here and let me see what you two look like in case something comes up missing."

Luscious and Déjà walked in the room and stood in front of her. She said as she looked at Luscious, "you the one my son sleeping with, I can tell. I can feel the spirit around you lusting for him."

Déjà thought to herself, *Oh my God, please don't tell me she's into this bullshit like Luscious.* Déjà looked around the room and to her horror she saw all the signs of voodoo: the dolls, books, chicken feet, etc. Déjà got a creepy feeling and told Luscious, "Let's get out of here," but it was too late. Luscious had already started a conversation with his mother about the practice of voodoo.

Luscious told the mother that Déjà was there to style hair and that she was a dancer there to choreograph a video for her son. The lady looked at Déjà and said, "Look on the dresser. Get my brush and pins and come show me what you can do."

Déjà didn't feel like doing it but Luscious wanted her to. She started brushing the lady's long, thick salt and pepper hair and listening to the conversation between her and Luscious. Déjà noticed all the pill bottles on the dresser and the machine and hospital bed. She assumed this lady was old and sick. But she seemed to be sharp in the mind. She spoke real slow and proper, with a slight accent, but Déjà couldn't place the accent. The lady was dark in color, kinda tall for a woman. She smelled like flower perfume and from the looks of her room and appearance, somebody was taking excellent care of her. She seemed to enjoy talking to Déjà and

Luscious. She gave Luscious some excellent advice. She said, "Although you're a beautiful woman you look like a whore. If you want anybody to take you seriously, you're going to have to cover all that up and act like a lady. She said to save all that sexy for the bedroom. She told Luscious maybe she should take an etiquette class.

Déjà fell out laughing and so did the old lady. But Luscious took her advice seriously. They lost track of time. It wasn't until the nurse came in to give her medicine that they rejoined the producer downstairs. He seemed a little disturbed about them talking to his mom. He said his mom suffered from nighttime dementia and shouldn't be disturbed. When the day was over they said their goodbyes and waited for the valet to bring them the car.

When the car pulled up Luscious grabbed her pepper spray and started cursing and looking for herbs in her purse. She started saying some weird stuff, like she was speaking in tongues, and throwing the herbs at the driver. It was then that Déjà realized it was Blue Eyes.

"What the fuck is going on?" the producer was screaming as he and his security were running to the driveway.

Luscious couldn't speak; she was stiff with fear. Déjà spoke up and told him all about Blue Eyes following Luscious around. The crazy part was when he called over his staff they didn't even know who Blue Eyes was, which was odd because he had on a valet uniform.

Luscious insisted that Déjà get in the car immediately. As they drove off Déjà looked back to see security had Blue Eyes jammed up. She looked up at the west wing window and saw the producer's mom in the window with what looked like a drawing of a crucifix made of pitchforks. When she told Luscious what she saw, Luscious seemed to gather comfort from that. She told Déjà it was a protection symbol. Déjà was uncomfortable with that. "Fucking weirdoes," she said under her breath.

Déjà checked her phone to see that the chief hadn't called her all day; as a matter of fact, it had been a few days since she'd heard from him. She was getting a little worried and a little pissed. However, she did have several calls from her young lover Ghost. As she listened to his messages she smiled and decided she would return them. She was going to call him tomorrow; that was number one on her to-do list.

When they pulled into Déjà's gated community the guards told her that someone just came looking for her. He said it was a Caucasian man with piercing blue eyes. Luscious just burst into tears. Déjà reassured her that most likely he wouldn't hurt her, but Déjà had her doubts. When they pulled into the driveway Déjà told Luscious to just spend the night because it was safer at her house. As they got out of the car and went into the house Déjà took a good look around. She saw nothing unusual. She locked the doors and turned on the alarm.

Seconds later the alarm went off. Déjà looked at the back door window; all she saw was Blue Eyes. It was too dark to see the face--only those eyes, blue as the sky. She grabbed her bat and ran to the backdoor. Blue Eyes ran toward the gate, with Déjà and her dog Kingsley in hot pursuit. Blue Eyes jumped in his car just in the nick of time because the dog was on his ass, and Déjà wasn't far behind with her Louisville slugger. He started up the car and tried to drive off but Kingsley was in the way. Déjà was screaming for the dog to move out of the way. "Move Kingsley, come here, boy."

She was screaming and before she knew it, Blue Eyes ran over Kingsley and kept on going. Déjà stopped in slow motion. She put her hands on her knees and tried to compose herself. She took one step forward and with her eyes filling with tears she tried to mutter, "Kingsley... " But nothing came out. She hesitantly walked over to her beautiful German shepherd lying there, hopeless and defenseless. Blood was pouring from his head and he was moving his hind legs and front legs, whining for help.

Tears rolled down Déjà's face as she reached in her pocket to get her cell to call 911. She begged and pleaded for the dispatcher to send an ambulance. As Kingsley lay there, barely holding on to life, the 911 dispatcher informed her that they didn't dispatch ambulances for nonhumans and connected her to Animal Control. Animal control was as helpful as they could be. Déjà was holding on to Kingsley's paw, rubbing his stomach just the way he liked. She said, "Hold on, buddy, help is in the way. I'm not going to let you die; hold on, fella."

Déjà's neighbor pulled up and said, "Let's take him to the emergency vet."

Déjà looked down at her four-legged best friend. He looked so helpless, not at all like the strong protector he had always been. She rubbed his paw and stroked his beautiful silky fur. She knew he was fading away. She sat next to him, holding his paw the entire time. She looked into his eyes, talking to him, and in the blink of an eye she saw the last twinkle of life leave his eyes. In a flash, he was gone.

Dog Killer

The scream Déjà gave was heartrending. Déjà screamed, "No, no, no, God no." She was hysterical with grief. She lay there in the middle of the street with Kingsley until Animal Control came to remove his lifeless body. Déjà sat on the curb for hours crying, until Chocolate pulled up with a bottle of Malibu Rum. Nothing was said; they just hugged and Déjà cried on Chocolate's shoulder and drank the Malibu Rum straight from the bottle. Chocolate helped her in the house and to the couch, where she passed out. Luscious was still sleeping in the oversized chair where she had drunk herself to sleep earlier. When Déjà awoke she heard voices and smelled food cooking. The first person she saw was Mama Pearly standing there with her arms stretched out to her. Déjà fell into them, crying uncontrollably--you know, that ugly cry where snot drips out of your nose and you keep sniffing. Mama Pearly was rubbing her back, telling her it was ok and that she was sure Kingsley went to dog heaven and he was chilling right now in a dog house made of gold, eating delicious dog bones and later he would run around in the biggest back yard imaginable, with plenty of beautiful redwoods for him to put his scent on. Déjà smiled at the thought of Kingsley running around dog heaven chasing messenger angels.

Luscious was awake and crying at the kitchen table, telling Déjà how sorry she was and that it was all her fault. Déjà could tell she felt just awful. Déjà and Luscious cried together and Déjà assured Luscious that this wasn't her fault.

"Hell," Déjà said, "you didn't know Blue Eyes was crazy." Déjà asked everybody how they knew what happened, because she hadn't called any one. They said that the neighbor had called Déjà's dad and he called Mama Pearly. Déjà's secretary set up a visit to some pet cemeteries for them to visit later, and he notified the doggie day care Kingsley attended twice a week of the situation. Kingsley used to attend the doggie day care Monday-Friday but the owner cut his hours because he said Kingsley had aggressive behavior issues and that he was probably suffering from anxiety separation. Chocolate always said that dog was crazy, just like Déjà. Anytime he was left alone too long he would tear up all the trash and drag it all through the house. That's why Déjà got the other smaller dog for him to play with. But Kingsley was wishy-washy; one day he liked her and the next day he didn't.

Déjà found the other dog outside in Kingsley's doghouse. She could sense something was wrong. Déjà sat down next to her and held her in her lap. She said, "Yeah girl, we both gonna miss him."

As Déjà walked Mama Pearly and Mr. Johnson to their car she noticed that all the neighbors on the street had their flags at half-mast. Mama Pearly said they all did it in honor of Kingsley. They all knew him because he often got loose and dug up all their flowers. Déjà smiled and hugged them goodbye. She had to pull herself together to get ready to go pick out dog caskets for Kingsley. As she turned she heard sirens and turned to see several police cars. She was confused at first; she thought to herself, *Damn, all these cars for my dog?"* Then she saw a familiar smile.

Chocolate was standing next to her. She said, "I called him. He hopped right in the car when he heard. He's been driving all night just to get to you--how about that?" Then she gave her a little push with her hip. She said, "I don't know too many men that would drive six hours nonstop because their--" she started to say girlfriend but stopped--"friend's dog got killed." Then she looked Déjà up and down and said, "Now you tell me who's got their priorities fucked up. While you wanting for that motha-fucka Ghost to get his shit together, you better get the one who's ready for you. Besides, you know you love him."

Déjà just frowned at Chocolate; she hated when she was right. Needless to say, Déjà was pleasantly surprised to see The Chief. He kissed her on the forehead and set his bags down. He said, "I came straight here. I'll take them to the room later."

Déjà picked his bag up and said, "No need to go to the room. I have plenty of room right here at Hotel Déjà. You're more than welcome to stay, and I heard the owner is super hot and sexy. If you're lucky, you just might get to sleep in the master suite."

They both smiled and embraced. Déjà melted into his arms. She missed him and from that tight hold he had on her, she knew he missed her too.

Chapter Seven

Goodbye Kingsley

117

Goodbye Kingsley

Déjà went upstairs to get dressed. She was dreading going to the pet cemetery, but she knew she had to do it. She grabbed some jeans and a top, then laid them on the bed. When she was getting panties out of the panty drawer she heard what sounded like gagging and crying coming from the bathroom. She hated when people used her upstairs bathroom. Hell that was her personal space and besides, there was a bathroom in the upstairs hallway and a bathroom downstairs. Why the fuck anybody felt the need to use her private bath room was a mystery to Déjà. She thought about getting it key coded. She laughed to herself and thought, *Naw, that's a little extreme.* She knocked on the bathroom door. "Who's in here?" Déjà opened the door before whoever was in there could reply. She saw Mama Pearly's granddaughter slumped over the toilet hurling up her entire breakfast. Déjà said, "Baby, what's wrong with you?" as she wiped her forehead with a cold, wet towel. The teenager sat up, barely able to lift her head. She started crying uncontrollably. Déjà thought, *Damn, everybody loves Kingsley so much.* Déjà tried to comfort the teenager by telling her the same thing Mama pearly told her about doggie heaven. That didn't seem to comfort her.

She looked up at Déjà and said, "Auntie, it's just a dog; you could get another one."

Déjà grasped for breath at what she said. *Little bitch,* Déjà thought. She said, "Well, if you feel like that then what the fuck you in my private bathroom crying like a little bitch for?" Then Déjà thought about something. She looked at her and said, "Stand up." Slowly the teenager stood up. Déjà got a good look at her. She said, "Let me get this shit straight: you in my private bathroom, throwing up and crying about something and obviously it ain't Kingsley, so what is it? And don't fucking lie." Déjà looked at her again and noticed something different. Normally the teenager had on tight-fitting clothes to show off her young, perfectly-shaped hourglass figure. But today she had on some loose fitting bullshit that wasn't even cute. "Raise up your shirt," Déjà asked her, then she put her hand on the teenager's stomach. Déjà closed her eyes and shook her head. She said, "Really, you know better than this. I took you to the clinic personally to get birth control. How did you let this happen? It's not like you don't know better. Besides, you know your crack-head mother is not gonna help you; hell, she don't even go visit her own son in the hospital. She's damn sure not going to support you having a baby." Déjà was going on and on about how irresponsible the teenager was until the girl burst out in tears and started throwing up again.

Déjà felt bad. She stopped lecturing her immediately. She went downstairs and got the teenager some ginger ale and crackers to calm her stomach. Everybody had left except Chocolate & the Chief. They were on the patio discussing how much Chocolate disliked the police and how unfair and prejudiced the entire judicial system was. Déjà dared not interrupt that conversation; hell, she felt the sameway. Never did she think she would be in love with an officer of the law, let alone a Chief of Police. She smiled at the thought of being in love with him. Then she made her way back upstairs to the pregnant teenager.

She said, "Here you go, Ratchet heffa." They both laughed. Deja thought she'd change her approach with her. She thought it would be best to stop criticizing her and hear her story of how this happened. Déjà took her to the other bedroom across the hall. As they talked, Déjà realized that the girl had been responsible. She said that the condom had burst and she didn't know until it was too late. Déjà asked her why she hadn't been taking her birth control pills and she responded by saying that her mother didn't turn in some form, which led to their public assistance getting cut off. At that point Déjà had heard enough. She told her that they would continue this conversation after the funeral.

The day of Kingsley's dog memorial finally came; it just so happened to be the day before the anniversary party. Déjà was dreading attending it; after saying goodbye to her dog she sure as the hell didn't want to go to some snobby party and pretend like her parents were the happiest couple when in actuality they were miserable. All of Déjà's close friends were there to support her (except for Chagita, who was still in Mexico). Déjà's assistant had put it all together. He had even blown a huge picture of Kingsley up and placed it on a holder outside in the back. They all said goodbye to him, even Déjà's dad, who felt like this was a waste of time. He said in his country they just buried dogs and moved on. The show stopper was when Mama Pearly rolled up after the services in a all white stretch Cadillac limousine. Déjà was just standing there looking at her and all her home girls from the church mothers' board. They were all dressed in white from head to toe. Déjà had to admit they all did look good, especially Mama Pearly, who had on a diamond-white two-piece skirt set, and her hat was to die for.

The Chief bent over to Déjà and said, "Now that's a little much for a dog funeral." Déjà laughed, then she saw the Pastor getting out of the car. The Chief shook his head. He looked at Déjà and said, "Really, what are they-- a gang of Christian riders?"

They both started busting up laughing. As they approached the house Déjà heard one of the mother board ladies say as she put her hand on Mama

Pearly's shoulder, "It's all right, sister. The Lord will help you through it, but at the same time take a little bit of this blessed oil and sprinkle it around you. You can't ever be too sure what kind of wickedness is lurking around these harlots."

Déjà frowned and laughed to herself. *That lady always did dislike us,* she thought to herself, ever since Chocolate got a ride from her husband years ago. She just assumed Chocolate was trying to seduce him. Little did she know Chocolate wasn't the one he wanted; it was Mama Pearly's thick ass he wanted. As they approached Déjà said, "Y'all didn't have to do all this for me."

Mama Pearly smiled and gave her a hug and proceeded into the house, but the mother board ladies couldn't let it go at that. One of them looked Déjà up and down and said real sarcastically, "We just came from a real funeral; one of the Lord's faithful servants was laid to rest. We went to pay our respects and let him know we were always going to remember him. Do you think we put on our Sunday best for this foolery? Child, please. The Lord takes care of his own and the devil takes care of the wicked! Now where's the bathroom and do you have seat covers, because ain't no telling who or what done been up and through here." Then, tightly holding on to her purse and trying not to touch anything, she brushed past Déjà in search of a bathroom.

Mother Pearlie looked back at Déjà and shook her head as she mouthed the words, "Let it go."

Déjà thought to herself if she wasn't scared of going to hell and burning in the flames she would have told that old bitch something. Chocolate gave her fake hellos, then she bent over and told Déjà, "Don't worry, I have some special cookies for their holier than thou asses," and she held up a bag of chocolate chip cookies she got from the medical weed store.

Déjà smiled and said, "Girl, you going to hell for sure." They both giggled.

After almost everybody was gone Déjà sprinkled his ashes in her rose bushes he loved so much. The mother board, after having several of Chocolate's famous cookies, had loosened up and was having an in-depth conversation with The Chief about the crime in California and if these trifling mamas would raise their kids and stay out of the clubs the world would be a better place, which was totally hilarious to Déjà because all the ones talking had the worst children. Déjà looked at Chocolate and said, "Bitch, I'm gon' pray for you."

Chocolate held up her hands and said, "Yes Lord, I receive it."

They both started laughing. One of the mother board ladies walked over to Déjà and said, "Honey, I don't know what in the world you did to deserve that man, but the Lord done sho-nuff blessed you with a good man." She pointed her finger at Déjà and said, "Baby, don't mess it up, 'cause I got three granddaughters and they'll snatch his behind up." She winked her eye at Déjà and walked away.

They were all over The Chief until he got a call from LAPD and he had to go. The Chief called her a few hours after he left and said he was on his way up the hill and that he had something she had to see. Déjà met him at the door. She couldn't believe it--why would he bring Blue Eyes to see her after he killed her beloved Kingsley? She ran over to punch him in the face but the Chief grabbed her arm and shouted, "No wait, listen to what he has to say."

Déjà folded her arms, smacked her lips and said, "I'm listening. Speak, dog killer." Déjà looked at Blue Eyes; it seemed like somebody had already whooped his ass. He had a black eye, broken leg, and if she wasn't mistaken he had what looked like serious burns on various parts of his body, including his arms and legs. He said first of all he was so sorry about Kingsley, but he had nothing to do with it. He said yes, he was at the house that night, but only to explain to Luscious how sorry he was for his behavior and to inform her that he would be checking himself into rehab for his prescription pain killer addiction and probably his sex addiction. He said he parked his car got out and was going to knock; however, he saw somebody headed around back. He said he followed and saw a medium-height, medium-weight man looking in the window at Déjà and Luscious. He pulled out his pepper spray and cell to call 911 but it was too late. He said the guy, who spoke in a Russian accent, pulled a gun on him and hit him in the eye with it. He said they scuffled but the guy got the best of him when he fell. He proceeded to say the guy forced him in the trunk of the car and then the next thing he knew the car was speeding off and he heard Déjà screaming to Kingsley to move. He said then the guy made a phone call, spoke in Russian, then poured gasoline over the car and set it on fire. He said he barely escaped alive and if it wasn't for the release button in the trunk, he would have been burned alive. Déjà stood there shaking in fear. She knew the Russian guy had found them. Blue Eyes said he had been in the burn unit for a week, and The Chief confirmed it. They didn't know who he was because his wallet got burned in the car fire and Blue Eyes passed out from smoke inhalation. The hospital notified the LAPD and they did a fingerprint scan to figure out who he was.

The entire time the Chief was checking Déjà out. He said, "Is there any reason why this Russian dude would spy on you and your friends?"

"Not that I'm aware of," Déjà responded.

The Chief looked at her hand said, "Ok" but didn't seem like he meant it.

Blue Eyes gave a whistle and out of The Chief's rental car jumped the most beautiful Alaskan husky Déjà ever saw. The dog walked right up to Déjà and looked up at her. First Déjà was a little scared, then the dog wagged its tail. Blue Eyes said, "Her name is Foxy. She wants to play with you."

Déjà gave Foxy a rub on the head. Foxy rubbed up against Déjà. Blue Eyes said, "See? She likes you." He told Déjà that since he got her dog killed, if she wanted she could keep Foxy. Or maybe she could keep her until he got out of rehab. Déjà was reluctant at first but then she agreed just until he got out of rehab. Foxy and Déjà walked back into the house and off went Blue Eyes and The Chief to the rehab, but not before The Chief told Déjà this conversation wasn't over.

When The Chief came back Déjà was upstairs talking to the pregnant teenager when Chocolate came upstairs and told her whatever they were talking about could wait, that Déjà needed to handle the situation that was brewing downstairs ASAP. Déjà saw Ghost standing at the bottom of the steps, and from the looks of it, he was pissed. When she got to the bottom of the steps she saw The Chief standing there looking. The Chief stuck out his hand as if to shake Ghost's hand and said, "What's up, big guy? I'm Eric."

Ghost looked The Chief up and down, not even acknowledging his presence. Ghost looked at Déjà and said, "Babe, let me talk to you. I didn't mean to bust up your party but you haven't returned my calls or texts, and I really need to talk to you."

Déjà was furious. How dare this arrogant motherfucker just bust all up in her house without calling and then demand she speak with him, and all in front of The Chief, like he didn't exist. Déjà said, "It's not a party; it's a funeral. Kingsley got ran over by a car and died." Then she pointed to the chief and said, "That's my friend Eric. I believe he was trying to speak to you."

Ghost looked over at The Chief and said very sarcastically, "What's up, man? You mind if I holla at Déjà for a minute? We have some unfinished business." He turned back and looked at Déjà and said, "Babe, I'm sorry about your dog. I know how much you loved him. Damn, I'm going to miss his bad ass getting loose and digging up all the neighbors' flowers."

At that point Chocolate grabbed her backpack. She looked at Déjà and said, "Cousin, you okay?"

Déjà replied, "Everything is cool."

The Chief walked outside, Chocolate and the pregnant teenager left and it was just Déjà and Ghost. Déjà looked at him and said, "Are you fucking

126

crazy? What's up with you demanding to speak with me? Just last week you was all up on Chocolate's auntie and then you was in love with some other bitch posting all over social media."

Then she walked to the door to see The Chief getting in his rental car. *Damn,* Déjà thought. She ran outside to the car. She said, "You don't have to leave."

The Chief didn't say a word; he just looked at her and drove off. Déjà stood there for a second, then she geared up to let Ghost have it.

When she got back in the house she found him in the kitchen eating leftover food from the funeral like he hadn't done a thing. Déjà looked at him sitting there looking sexy as hell. She sat across from him and said, "What's your problem, dude?"

He looked up and said, "I'm in love with you and you're in love with me. Simple as that, and you know it."

Déjà closed her eyes and held her breath for a second. She said, "I'm seeing The Chief and he's a good man."

He said, "But you don't love him like you love me, and you know it. If you did I wouldn't be sitting here eating. You would have got all kinds of ghetto hood crazy with me as soon as you saw me."

Déjà hated the fact that he was right. "What about Chocolates aunt and the heffa you posted about?"

Goodbye Kingsley

He looked at Déjà. "What about her? She's cool but she ain't you, and I only posted that because I knew your spying ass was stalking my page instead of just calling me." Then he went on to tell Déjà how he had to move out of his place because the building went into foreclosure. He asked her if he could crash on her sofa for a few days, until his new place was ready.

Déjà just looked at him, then her phone buzzed. Ghost mumbled something smart ass like, "Probably your lame-ass dude."

Déjà picked up the phone to read the text: "I think it's best if you and I are friends. You have a lot going on in your life, some of which may be illegal, and since I'm The Chief of police, I really don't want to get involved, plus it seems like you and the gentleman have some unfinished business. I wish you well." Déjà couldn't believe this shit; this motherfucker was sending her a breakup text when they weren't even officially an item. What the fuck? Déjà was a little hurt but not really; hell, she was sitting across from this young, handsome fellow who she obviously had feelings for.

Déjà rolled her eyes at Ghost and handed him a blanket out of the hallway closet. He tried to explain to her what happened between him and Chocolate's aunt but Déjà just rolled her eyes, put up her hands and said, "No need to explain." Hell, Déjà knew Chocolate's aunt like the back of her hand; no explanation needed. She had a banging body and spit game like a nigga. But she liked to get high on more than weed and once Ghost found out, he was out. He hated women who drank and smoked; his mom was on drugs for most of his childhood, so any woman who remotely reminded him of her was not an option.

Goodbye Kingsley

Ghost just looked at Déjà and smiled. He walked up on her and slowly put his arms around her. He said, "You know you broke my heart when you told me I was too young and you didn't want me. But the way you showed out when you saw me in the back yard proved what I already knew: you love me like I love you." He kissed Déjà on the back of her neck slowly.

She moved away and said, "On the sofa you go, smart ass; a few nights and your ass is out of here. Besides, I'm sure you had a number of places to go."

"Thanks Ms Lady," he replied, "but if you get scared upstairs in that king size bed alone just holla."

Déjà looked at him and said, "I'll be okay."

He said, "But I can make you feel better than okay."

Déjà turned around and said goodnight as she walked upstairs. After she got herself washed up and into her pajamas she called Chocolate to let her know everything was cool. She thought about calling The Chief but hell, what was the point? He said everything he had to say in his text. She went downstairs to turn on the alarm and found Ghost watching a movie and eating some more food in his t-shirt and drawers. He had put all the food away and straightened up the kitchen. She went to the back door to let the little dog in. She didn't want her outside with that new dog Foxy. As she called for her, she accidentally called her Kingsley. Déjà just burst into tears.

Ghost walked over and put his arms around her. He said, "Come lay with me for a while." Déjà was so upset she laid on the sofa in his arms and fell asleep. She woke up screaming and crying a few hours later. She felt Ghost grab her. He said, "It's okay, babe, you just dreaming."

She looked at him. She was hysterical with grief. She said, "I dreamed you got married to some awkwardly-shaped lady and invited me to the wedding. I was all dressed up but you didn't even notice me." She continued to say that the lady and he were so in love but couldn't afford a ring so they exchanged gold hoop earrings and for a wedding gift he gave her True Religion jeans. She started crying even harder when she described their wedding cake. She said at the reception he and the lady were dressed alike in jeans and printed shirts with their pictures on them. Ghost smiled. He wiped the tears from Déjà's eyes and said, "Babe, if I marry anybody, it's going to be you, plus when I get married I'm damn sure going to be able to afford a nice ring."

Déjà laughed and then she kissed his lips. As she observed him catching a quick cat nap after their first round of intense lovemaking, she thought to herself how much she really had missed him. Months had passed since she'd last been with him. In that moment it felt like it had just been yesterday. The way he made her feel was unlike no other. The way he held and caressed her hadn't changed. He always made her feel like she was the only woman in the world. She stared at him, gently running her fingers across his freshly lined goatee. She kissed his lips while he slept. She didn't want to wake him because she wasn't ready yet for another round. She knew if she woke him that's exactly what would happen. She tried to put her finger on what exactly it was about him that drove her so crazy. It wasn't the fact that he was extremely handsome, but that didn't hurt either. It wasn't the fact that when he smiled at her it sent chills down her spine.

Goodbye Kingsley

It wasn't anything that he had or did for her. It wasn't the fact that he was extremely spiritual, although sometimes he did get on her nerves. He had a smart-ass mouth sometimes and was always quoting Bible verses at her at the wrong times. She always thought, *Why he gotta bring Jesus in this?* If not for her fear of the Almighty she would have said something like, "Those are the same Bible verses the master used to quote to the slaves, right before they whipped, tortured, raped and dehumanized them." She knew that would send him into a frenzy but her intense fear of God was greater than her need to antagonize him. Hell, that would just be another thing she had to answer to God for, and her list was already long enough. Basically, she thought to herself, it was just the chemistry they shared--the way they just seemed to connect without even saying a word. It was his kind spirit, laid back attitude, and his ability to always see the good in any situation: that's what she loved about him. She laid her head on his heart and listened to it beat softly. She was feeling a certain type of way, sort of like she'd dropped the ball on this situation. She started to think that maybe they were meant to be together. Maybe God sent him to her to nurture, guide and bring him into a loving family and love him. In return, he would provide, protect, be the reason she kept her legs closed to the creeps she'd been so promiscuous with in the past and love her. She didn't know the reason he'd brought him back in her life but she was grateful.

She felt his hand rubbing the lower part of her back and ass cheeks. She was ready for another round. She kissed his lips, neck, chest, and below his waist. She knew she had it right when he closed his eyes and dropped his head to the side. He let out a low moan but he was too manly to moan for real. That's okay; she knew he enjoyed it. She gently climbed on him and lined her body parts up with his. He helped her slide down slow on him. It was a little painful--that good kind of pain. He squeezed her around the waist as she slowly rode him. She whispered in his ear all the things she'd wanted to say a long time ago, like how she loved him, how she hated seeing him with somebody else and how she always felt like he was hers. She told him she always wanted to tell him that. He gently held her face, looked her in the eyes and said, "It's okay, you can tell me now," then he pushed all the way inside her. She grabbed for the sofa arm to hold onto, but he had flipped her over to a new position. His tongue was on her clitoris, one hand caressing her nipples and the other hand inside her--well, only his fingers but his hands were so big it felt like he was still inside her. She thought her heart was going to explode through her ribcage she was breathing and screaming so loud. He went inside her as he held both her legs wide open. He licked her legs and bit her slightly as he went deeper and deeper inside her.

When she awoke the next morning she found the little dog standing by her with her head slightly twisted, giving Déjà that judgmental look. Déjà swore that dog was human in a past life. She picked her up and said, "Don't judge me, bitch. I haven't forgotten your indiscretion with the poodle down the street." Déjà found Ghost outside smoking a cigarette and reading the paper with Foxy sitting at his feet.

He said, "I already fed them and took them for a walk."

Déjà thought that was amazing since she never walked her; she just opened the back door and let her out.

He looked at Déjà. "Are you okay? I didn't mean to take advantage of you, but you started it with that kiss. Was that just because you were pissed with that ole dude, The Chief?"

Déjà replied, "Not at all." They both smiled.

He said, "Well. today is Saturday. Do you have any plans?"

Déjà remembered the anniversary party was tonight. She felt her stomach go queasy over the thought of going. She asked Ghost if he had a suit and if so, would he accompany her to the anniversary party. He reluctantly agreed and told her he would meet her at the party. He said he had some business to take care of and that he also had to leave at 10pm because he worked night shift at UPS now.

Déjà smiled. She said, "What, you got a job? Good for you."

He smiled and said, "Yeah, it's just a warehouse job."

Déjà replied, "A job is a job; if the check has your name on it, you good."

He smiled and asked, "Towels in the bathroom?"

Déjà nodded her head yes and walked in the kitchen to make some coffee. She got a call from Chagita letting her know she was back in the States and that she would be at the anniversary party tonight. Déjà could tell by the tone of Chagita's voice something was troubling her. When Déjà tried to discuss the recent events and ask about John Paul, Chagita simply replied she was over it and she didn't want to discuss it anymore. When Déjà continued to discuss the situation, Chagita politely told Déjà she'd see her tonight and not to worry about her because she was fine; that part of her life was over. Déjà hung the phone up.

Goodbye Kingsley

Ghost walked in the kitchen to find Déjà in deep thought. He said, "Babe, you ok?"

She just nodded her head yes. He told her to let him make some calls and he would stay with her all day, until the anniversary party. They spent the afternoon together just lounging around the house. It was a perfect day to lounge, as it was pouring down rain outside, which Déjà took as a clear warning tonight was going to be a disaster. She had a sick feeling all day.

Déjà's assistant came over with Déjà's dress that she had delivered to her office but she wasn't there to receive it because of her dog's funeral. As he walked in he said, "Hey Ms. Thang what's up with that glow?"

At that very moment Ghost emerged from the kitchen. The assistant looked him up and down. He smiled and looked over at Déjà and back at Ghost. He said, "Oh my, and who might this beautiful specimen be?" Then he put his hands together as if he was praying and said, "Dear Lord, I knew when you wanted me to go out in the pouring, wet, cold rain, and drive twenty miles to bring Ms. Thang her dress there was going to be a blessing in it for me. Thank you, Lord."

Déjà could tell that Ghost was uncomfortable with her assistant. Déjà told her assistant to back off. They both laughed and the assistant looked at Ghost and said, "Please tell me you're not one of those homophonic black men who think all gay men want them?"

Ghost just stood there at a loss for words. He looked at Déjà and said, "Babe, I'm going to get dressed and meet you there because remember, I have to leave early because of work."

Goodbye Kingsley

Déjà replied, "You're gonna ride that motorcycle in all this pouring rain?"

He said, "Yeah babe, I'm good. I'm a big boy; I can handle it."

Déjà's assistant couldn't help but add to that statement. He looked at Ghost and said, "Yes, I'm sure you are; just make sure you always wear your helmet."

Ghost looked at Déjà. He said, pointing to Déjà's assistant, "Babe, really?"

Déjà once again told her assistant to behave then offered one of her cars to Ghost to use that night for work. Ghost refused and started walking upstairs to get ready. As he was walking away the assistant said his goodbyes then shouted out loud enough for Ghost to hear, "A little wetness never hurt nobody," then he looked at Déjà and said, "Ms. Thang, if I had that delicious piece of man candy upstairs, I'd say to hell with that party and put on my sexiest lingerie and go lick my candy until I found out how many licks it took me to get to the center." He winked his eye at her and said, "Know what I'm saying?" Then he started singing, "It's raining men."

Déjà laughed, pushed him out the door and locked the door, then proceeded up the steps when she decided to take a second look out the glass door. She saw an unfamiliar car outside but just dismissed it as a neighbor having company.

Chapter Eight

The Anniversary Part One

The Anniversary Part One

As Déjà drove into the driveway of her parent's home she observed all the fancy cars and the valet parking. Inside she saw all the waiters wearing tuxedos and white gloves serving appetizers and champagne. She quickly grabbed a glass because she knew it was going to be a long night. When she saw her mother standing at the top of the staircase with that full length sequined gold strapless evening dress on, she guzzled another glass of wine. She hated to admit it but her mother did look fabulous and that up hairdo she was rocking was beautiful. Déjà couldn't have done it better herself. That was one thing good Déjà could say about her mother: although she was an evil, sadistic, rotten to the core bitch, she was always polished and well put together, from head to toe. And she had a shape and bone structure to die for. That was the one thing that always puzzled Déjà. Her mom was tall, dark brown, and thinly built.

But Déjà was the opposite: she was short, light brown, and curvy. They often said she took after her father's side of the family but she didn't see resemblance since her dad was also tall and dark. Women loved her dad; he was smooth. He had a way with them and that African accent, those tribal markings on his face, and the fact that he was rich sealed the deal. Déjà saw him standing in the corner trying to be social. He hated gatherings and being around a lot of people. He was a recluse and enjoyed spending time alone with his family.

Déjà's mother was the opposite; she loved being in the spotlight and showing off all she had. And they had a lot: property, investments, dental practice-- the list went on and on. Plus Déjà's mother was a successful doctor, which she let you know every chance she got. She loved to brag about what she had and the gifts her husband gave her, just like she was doing all night with that ten carat platinum anniversary band Déjà's dad

139

had given her. Well, at least that's what her mom was saying. Déjà knew damn well her dad didn't pick that out, nor did he care about this anniversary party. He probably had given her his credit card and told her to buy whatever it was she wanted. And this anniversary party surely was Déjà's mama idea. Her daddy didn't even love her mom. But Déjà's mama loved to keep up appearances with her high society friends.

Déjà didn't understand why her parents stayed together. When she and her brother were little her dad said he was staying for them. But now they were well past grown so why he stuck around was a mystery to her. She walked over and gave her dad a kiss. "Hey old man," Déjà said as she kissed him.

"Baby girl, are you enjoying yourself?" he asked, laughing. He knew they both hated her mom's boring parties.

Déjà introduced Ghost to her father as her friend. They shook hands and her Dad said, "You must be pretty special because baby girl never brings home her boyfriends."

They both laughed. He lifted his drink up and pointed to the door and said, "I see your cousin and your friends made it."

Chocolate, Luscious and Chagita had arrived together. *Thank God,* Déjà thought. *My support team is here to get me through the night.* Déjà was still waiting on Soni Lynn and her family. Déjà had invited them so she could meet Soni Lynn's mom, whom Soni Lynn spoke so highly of. Déjà was a little jealous; she wished her and her mom had that relationship. Soni Lynn and Déjà were becoming good friends, even though Soni Lynn was about nine years younger. Déjà liked her spunk and took her in under her wing like a little sister.

Chocolate had on her usual misguided attire, Chagita looked beautiful as always, but Déjà was pleasantly surprised and also a little disappointed with Luscious' wardrobe selection. It always gave Déjà great satisfaction to watch her mother squirm and panic as she watched Déjà's brother check out all Luscious' assets. Déjà's mother loathed Luscious. She said she was a no-good tramp whose only goal in life was to seduce and trap successful men. This couldn't be farther from the truth. Déjà stared at Luscious for a while. She couldn't remember the last time she saw her with all her wiggly parts covered. Luscious looked like a beautiful vision in a beautiful form-fitting caramel colored satin gown trimmed in gold. And even though she was completely clothed you couldn't help but notice her exquisite shape. Déjà couldn't help but wonder if that amazingly handsome specimen of a man whose arm she was holding had anything to do with this drastic change in appearance, or was it his mother's blatant advice. Every since Luscious started dating him her wardrobe started shifting for the better. He somehow convinced her she was beautiful and more appealing fully clothed. He convinced her that men wanted to imagine what was under her clothes, not see everything upfront. Plus Déjà could tell Luscious was falling for him.

Déjà had to admit she was glad she invited Ghost. However, she didn't want her mother getting her hands on him; hell, it was almost ridiculous that her ex was here. Déjà knew her mom invited him just to aggravate her. Déjà thought she'd wait a while before she spoke to him; hell, if she would even speak at all was still up for debate.

The Anniversary Part One

Déjà's mom made her way over to Déjà and Ghost. Déjà just knew she was going to have something judgmental to say about him. She gave Déjà the usual once-over, then the fake hug and kiss. She even complimented Déjà's dress, although she did throw in a jab. She said "it's kinda tight though; maybe it would fit better if you lost a few pounds."

Ghost stepped in and said, "Well, I don't think she needs to lose not one pound. She looks beautiful to me."

Déjà introduced him to her mom; to Déjà's surprise she seemed to like him. She even complimented him on how handsome he was. Then she went in for the kill, shooting off a round of personal questions like "where do you live, what do you do, and where did you go to college" But Ghost was a smooth talker and answered them all with charm. Déjà's mom was a big flirt herself; she came back with, "Oh my, you're a laborer. What would we do without you guys?" Then she looked at Déjà and back at Ghost and said, "Well, make sure you eat all you can and feel free to take some home. I'm sure you're starving; my daughter has never been a good cook."

Ghost replied, "No ma'am, quite the contrary, she always makes my favorites." (Which was hilarious to Déjà and Ghost because his favorite was hot dogs and pork and beans, something he often made for himself as a child when his mom was out getting high).

She smiled then made a frown when she saw Chocolate walking past. She walked away to socialize with her guests. As usual Chocolate headed straight for the bar. She said if she had to put up with this bullshit she was going to at least have several drinks. Déjà agreed and all the girls began to drink heavily. As the waiters walked around passing out delicious treats, Déjà accidentally bumped into one. Luckily she didn't spill her platter. Déjà grabbed the waitress by the arm and said, "I'm so sorry, are you okay?" Then Déjà recognized the waitress. It was the stripper from the Wet Kitty, one of Lucas's whores.

The waitress looked shocked that Déjà had been so nice to her. Then she said, "Next time you should watch where you're going" and rolled her eyes and walked off.

Déjà just shook her head. *Ignorant bitch,* Déjà thought. All the ladies started teasing Déjà, saying if they were her they wouldn't take anything off her tray because she was definitely spitting in it! They started laughing and drinking more. After they had drinks, Ghost kissed Déjà goodbye and left for work.

Déjà finally made her way over to speak to her ex. They had a brief conversation about how nice the party was. As Déjà walked away she saw something odd: an angry white lady walking really fast toward her, dragging a little girl by the hand. When she got closer Déjà realized it was the bitch that broke up her relationship with her ex. *What the fuck is she doing here?* Déjà said to herself. She walked up to Déjà, screaming something about she was tired of Déjà always up in her man's face and why didn't she just leave them alone and let them be happy. Déjà knew she had lost it.

Déjà said, "Are you fucking retarded? You don't have a relationship with him, stupid; you got fucked, got pregnant and that's the extent of your so-called relationship; now get the hell out of my parent's home ruining their anniversary party."

By that time they had gained an audience and Déjà's ex was rushing toward them. He said, "Stop it; you're making a scene" and he grabbed the white lady by the arm and tried to pull her away.

She refused to go. She said, "I followed you here. I knew you was coming to meet your slut; you don't care about me or the baby." Then she burst into tears, screaming about child support and how she loved him. It was an awful scene, especially considering the fact that they had never been a couple and he had a restraining order on her, not to mention the fact that their baby she was referring to was now six years old.

He said as he pointed to the door, "Leave right now or I'm going to have you arrested."

That sent her over the edge. She went completely ballistic, screaming about how she was his only child's mother and a bunch of other nonsense. Déjà's mom was furious. She had security escort her to the downstairs guest room until she calmed down, then she insisted she leave. She turned around and gave Déjà the coldest stare. She said, "It's bad enough you have all your misfit friends here. But to start a scene with these good people is UN-acceptable," then she turned around to ask Déjà's ex if he was okay. Before Déjà could say a word her mom walked off with him.

The little girl was standing there looking at Déjà. Déjà said, "Are you okay sweetie?"

The little girl looked Déjà up and down. She said, "You don't look like a monster bitch."

Déjà stepped back; she couldn't believe what she heard she said. "Excuse me missy, what did you say?"

The little girl looked up at her with her big green eyes and said, "My mom said she was coming to the party to confront the monster bitch that's keeping us from being a family. I'm guessing that's you because I've seen pictures of you at my father's house and my mom was screaming at you. But you don't look like a monster bitch. You're actually really pretty."

Déjà smiled and thought to herself, *A smart ass just like her father.* Déjà said, "Sorry to disappoint you."

The little girl replied, "I'm not disappointed. Besides, I know it's not you keeping us from being a family; it's my mom. My dad says she crazy."

Déjà smiled and said, "I think your daddy hit the nail on the head with that. You know your daddy loves you very much."

The little girl said, "Yes I do; he tells me all the time, but I think he loves you too."

Déjà bent down at eye level to the little girl. She hugged her and said, "You're such smart little girl and your daddy was right; your mother is nuts." Then she grabbed the little girl by the hand and said, "Come on, let me get you to your dad before I have to whoop your crazy mama's ass."

As they walked through the party she saw Soni Lynn and her family. Soni

The Anniversary Part One

Lynn had brought her handsome brother Xavier, whom Déjà had already met a few weeks ago at the office, as well as her mother and her stepfather, who was also handsome. *Damn,* Déjà thought, *what a cute family. The mama's cute the daddy is cute and the kids are cute.* Déjà walked over and hugged Soni Lynn. She said, "I see you made it." Then she looked at Soni Lynn's mother she said, "You must be her sister because you're way too young to be her mother."

Soni Lynn's mother said, "Hello, I'm Mary and this is my husband Romello and this is my son Xavier, and yes, I had them when I was ten."

They both smiled and Déjà stuck out her hand to shake Mary's. She said, "Hello, I'm Déjà," but instead of Mary shaking her hand, she put her arms around her and hugged her.

Then Mary looked at the little girl standing there with Déjà. "What a pretty little doll baby you are." Then she looked at Déjà and said, "Does she belong to you?"

Déjà frowned and said, "Not hardly."

Then the little girl said, "My mom is the crazy white lady in the guest room lying down. She didn't take her medicine today and she started a fight with Ms. Déjà now we have to leave."

Déjà jerked the little girl's hand and said, "You don't have to tell everything. Now let's find your daddy."

Mary smiled. She said, "Oh my, then I guess we'll see you later."

Déjà said, "It was nice to meet you, Mary and family." She looked at Soni Lynn and said, "We will have to do lunch before your family leaves back for Harlem."

"Of course," Soni Lynn responded. She looked at her mother Mary and said, "Is that cool, Mommy?"

"Yes, of course. We'll bring your granny Suga Bell, too."

Déjà said, "Yes, I'm dying to meet her. Soni Lynn tells stories about her all the time."

The little girl looked at Mary, then at Deja. She said, "Are you guys sisters? You look alike."

Déjà replied, "No, we're not sisters." They chatted a few minutes more, then Déjà spotted her secretary. She said as she handed the little girl to him, "Please find her dad and give her to him; the last time I saw him he was headed toward the deck with the wicked witch of Baldwin hills."

"No, no, Miss Thang, I don't do children! Nope, not me," he said as he handed her back to Déjà.

"Please," Déjà asked.

"Sorry, can't be a part of that," he responded.

Then the little girl said to him, "Are you one of those homosexuals?" Déjà's secretary was floored. He said, "Why yes, I am, little girl, and what do you know about homosexuals, if I may ask?"

"Yes you may ask," she said. "I just know God made Adam and Eve not Adam and Steve--at least, that's what my daddy says, and he also said that homosexuals complain way too much and just want the whole world to be gay."

Déjà closed her eyes, put her hand over her heart, took a deep breath and said, "Let me get this girl to her daddy."

Déjà's secretary said, "Yes, please do that before she gets body slammed! She's just as crazy as her mammy," then he stormed off. Déjà knew he was livid.

Finally she found the little girl's father outside. Everybody had gathered outside to cut the cake, but first they had to view home videos of Déjà's family. Her mother played these home videos at every party, except now she had gotten all high tech and had all them put on flash drives that she could play from any computer. This time she had a wide hundred inch screen to watch them on. Before they watched the videos, Déjà's mother gave a big speech on how lucky she was to have been married for thirty-five years and how she and Déjà's father were so happy. Déjà stopped listening halfway through the speech because she knew it was bullshit. Her mom and daddy barely spoke and slept in different rooms. How much happiness was that?

Chapter Nine

The Anniversary Part Two

The Anniversary Part Two

Lucas finally showed up and was scoping out the single ladies. Déjà, Chocolate, Lucas and Luscious all sat at the same table with Soni Lynn and her family. Déjà was looking for Chagita. Déjà had been watching Chagita all night; she was acting very strange. Déjà wondered if it was just because of the information she learned or if it was more. Déjà found Chagita outside sitting by the rose gardens, looking confused. She was so far into thought that she didn't even notice Déjà walk over and sit next to her. "Hey chica, what's up with you? Why the gloomy face? It's a party with free food, free entertainment, and all the free liquor you can drink! You should be smiling about the liquor alone. You know how you love to drink!"

Chagita gave a half-fake smile and continued to stare off into Neverland.

"Ok Heffa, spill it. What the fuck happened in Mexico?"

Chagita's eyes welled up with tears as she burst out, "I did it."

"You did what?" Déjà asked, confused.

After she sobbed uncontrollably Chagita calmed down and began to tell her story. "When I was in Mexico I persuaded John Paul with sex (she added how she was so good at it to the story; Déjà just ignored that. Plus she mentioned the little trick she did with her tongue. Déjà also ignored that because she knew she was putting a thousand on that, anyway) to tell me the location of the monster who attacked my family. With great hesitation he told me the monster's location. He said he was gravely sick with lung disease and was in hiding at a monastery deep in the mountains in Mexico. It took me three days to drive there. When I got there I dressed

151

in a nurse's uniform to get in. I found him in his room alone and praying to the Virgin Mary for forgiveness of his sins. I slowly approached him and removed the scarf I'd tied around my face.

"He took a deep breath. He wasn't shocked to see me and he knew exactly who I was. He said, 'Your face is the face that haunts my dreams; the sound of your cries fills my thoughts and takes my breath away. I've spent many sleepless nights praying to the father to take me and end my torment.' His fragile hands turned up the oxygen pump that was connected to him. He looked weak and tired, not at all like the monster he once was. He used to be tall, slim, nice looking. But then again, all evil people are beautiful on the outside; that's how they lure you in. 'When I saw you on the beach I knew you would come for me. I've been waiting for you.'

"'Well, your wait is over. You are a horrible person. You don't deserve to be here on earth for what you've done!' His reply, to my surprise, was that he was in total agreement with me. He begged me to have a seat and listen to him; he said I could call it his last rites.

"Reluctantly, I agreed because I wasn't quite sure how I was going to kill him, but I was quite certain that day was going to be his last. I sat in the chair next to his bed while he told his story. He said as a child he was privileged from birth; he never wanted for anything. His every want was catered to by his nannies, maids and servants. He said he developed a taste for death, people suffering, ruling over people and having his way. He said he didn't understand why, that it was just the way he was. He said his mom said he was born evil; that when he was a baby he had black, soulless eyes. He said his mom became fearful of him in his teenage years, after he killed the family pets. She said she could see the devil in him and sent him away to boarding school. When he was of age and a college graduate, his father died and the family said it was time for him to take over the family business. Quickly he learned that the family business was robbing, stealing, drug dealing, and killing--all the things he said he was good at. Soon everyone in the town feared him and he ruled over everyone and everything in it.

"He continued to say that he met a beautiful young virgin from Belize and married her and had five sons with her, all of which he was grooming to take over his business when they were of age. I didn't say a word; I just listened. 'On the day I had come to your house to pay a visit and collect from your family, my wife informed me that she never loved me; that she only married me in fear for her life. She revealed to me that my very touch made her sick to her stomach and she despised all the devil sons she had borne me because they were evil just like me. She said she wanted to leave but she knew I wouldn't let her go. She was right about that. I was already spiraling out of control and your fathers' words stung my soul. I knew he was everything I was not: good, respectable, righteous, and honest--all qualities I'd never possess. That day in my heart of hearts I knew I was wrong, but the evil that lived inside of me filled my mind.'

"He paused for a second and looked into my eyes. He said, 'My wife I loved, but I treated her like everyone else, like trash beneath my feet. In my old years I've come to realize that I never felt worthy to be loved because of the monster that lives inside of me.'"

Chagita said she asked one question. "Your wife--what happened to her?"

"Karma is what happened to her!" he replied as he gasped for air. Tears streamed down his face. That was the first time she felt the slightest bit of sympathy for him. She knew he was a wicked person but she could feel the love he had for his wife. He caught his breath and held his heart as he said, "The coroner said at the exact time I ordered all your family members dead, my beloved wife took the lives of my four youngest sons with a single gunshot wound to the head as they slept. Then she pointed the gun at her face and blew it off. In her suicide note she said it was her beauty and brown skin that attracted the devil in me, so by her destroying the very thing I loved about her, in her death I could not build a shrine around her." He took a breath. "She knew me so well." Chagita said she thought, *That's what he gets* and didn't feel sorry for him. His wife was right; he was the devil. The only thing was, she said he told her he had five sons. She said she asked him what happened to the fifth son? Why didn't she kill him? Chagita said he sat up coughed up some blood. After he cleaned himself up he said, "My oldest son, who is the mirror image of his mother both in appearance and mannerisms, was working with me that day. I'd forced him to become part of my organization and he hated me for it. He wanted to be a priest and save the world; he was full of bright ideas and hope for the future, and I crushed all his hopes and dreams by trying to make him into a killer, but the boy wasn't cut out for it. He was too righteous, so I made him my driver and in doing so he witnessed every monstrous thing I did. The killings, the drug dealing, my whores--you name it, he saw it, even the slaughter of your family at my command." Chagita said she damn near fainted; she stood up, gasping for air. She said she slowly said, "John Paul?"

He looked at her, smiled and said, "The only good thing I've ever done. His mother named him after Pope John Paul the first. He has forgiven me for all my sins and so has The Lord my God, whom I took a vow of silence for. I haven't spoken in eighteen years until this day. The Lord sent you to me to redeem my wicked ways, after I found my wife and children dead. The coward in me wanted to take my own life. I could not live with the shame and hurt over losing them. I picked the gun up and aimed it for my heart because when she killed herself I had nothing to live for. However The Lord felt that I hadn't suffered enough for my crimes so I missed my heart by a couple of inches and those holier than thou doctors saved my sorry ass to live another day to suffer here by myself. So on this day if you've come to take me out, be my guest. I'm ready to go."

Chagita said she didn't know what to say and his sad story didn't discount the fact he'd murdered everybody she loved. Chagita said he looked at her and screamed, "Get on with it, foolish little girl, kill me, send me to the saints—please, put me out of my misery."

Chagita said she'd thought about letting him live to let the torture of his soul continue but the rage she had for him couldn't be contained. She said she simply unplugged his breathing machine. At first he didn't fight back; he just looked at her, ready to die. Then he grabbed her arm and she told him, "God may forgive your sorry ass for your sins but I most certainly do not. I hope you burn in the everlasting flames of hell." She said she felt the life slipping from his body. After it was done she simply put on her head scarf and walked away.

Déjà was at a loss for words. She just sat there, confused. She couldn't believe that her best friend of eighteen years just told her she knowing and willingly killed a person. For a quick second Deja thought Chagita had been watching way too many TV crime shows. The tension was thick and Déjà knew she was going to have to do something to break the tension so they could figure out a plan to keep Chagita out of some Mexican prison. So Déjà simply said, "Please tell me the sex with John Paul was amazing, toe curling, mind blowing, can't breathe sex?"

Chagitas smile from ear to ear, showing all thirty-two teeth answered that. Déjà put her arms around Chagita and said, "Come on, little killer, we got to get you together." Déjà knew this was going to be one of those secrets she went to her grave with, even if it was from a jail cell shared with Chagita.

As Déjà and Chagita walked back to the party they saw everybody standing there staring at the screen like they had seen a ghost. Most of the people couldn't take their eyes off it. Then they heard the music. Déjà was a little shocked; she'd never heard her mom listening to rap music. As they got closer her eyes focused on the screen. Her mouth dropped open and her heart sank down to her knees. Somehow, somebody had taped the little strip show she put on down at the Wet Kitty that day Lucas' ex pissed her off. Now it was playing for all her parents' family and close friends to see. Déjà nearly fainted. Her dad ordered the technician to turn it off but he said he didn't know where the feed was steaming from.

Then, to top all that off, Déjà's ex's crazy baby mama came screaming in the back yard and pointing to Déjà, saying she told them Déjà was a home-wrecking whore. Before Déjà could get to her, Chocolate jumped on her and whooped her ass. It took two men to pull Chocolate off her. It was a mess.

Déjà's mom was mortified, especially when she heard one of her guests say to her husband to hurry up and get her out of this party before it turned into ones of those swinger parties he was always trying to take her to. Then she looked at Déjà's mom and said, "It's okay if you're into that, but as for me and my husband, we aren't."

The part that really sent Déjà's mom into overdrive is when the lady told her to take her off any future guest lists, because she and her husband didn't associate with people like her. Déjà's dad was just sitting at the table with his head down, finishing his drink. Déjà knew it was just a matter of time before her mom dug into her. Déjà's brother's advice to her was to leave before she could start. However, Déjà felt just awful so she went to her mom to apologize after the last guest had left. Not that Déjà was embarrassed of what she had done, because she wasn't. She felt bad that her parents were embarrassed and that their party was ruined. She really couldn't care less what anyone thought about her, especially those uptight, snotty, fake ass people.

She looked at Déjà and said, "Look what you did; you bought shame upon this house. You're a filthy slut just like your mother." Then she smacked her across the face. Déjà stood there for a second. She was confused because if she wasn't mistaken, she was her mother. Déjà's older brother took a deep breath and put his hand over his mouth, as if he was shocked his mother said that.

Her daddy looked at her mother with disgust. He put his finger in her face and said, "Don't you ever mention her again. She was an angel compared to you; you are the devil."

Before they knew it he had smacked her clear across the table and she went flying into the china cabinet. The older brother had to pull him off her. The daddy was screaming "murderer" in Swahili.

Déjà just stood there confused. She thought, *What the hell is going on?* She looked at her dad standing there crying and looking like he was in deep thought. "What is Mommy talking about?"

"Leave it alone, baby girl," her dad replied. He put his hand on her shoulder, gave her the saddest look she had ever seen and walked to his office, as if his whole world had been crushed.

Déjà looked at her older brother. "What are they talking about?"

He just stood there in a trance. With tears in his eyes, he said, "You are my little sister and I love you with all my heart. I always have and always will. I've always tried to protect you." He looked down at the ground, "Little sister, this is one I can't protect you from." Then he looked at their mother and said, "Wicked woman." He gathered up his wife and left.

Déjà stood there trying to put what just happened together. She always felt as if her mother hated her, but tonight her mother confirmed it. The look in her mother's eyes was pure, unmistakable hatred. Déjà looked at her mother with tears rolling down her face and said, "Are you saying you're not my mother?"

Her response was cold as ice. "I could never birth something as filthy as you; I hope your whore-bitch mother is burning in hell." Then she walked off.

Chocolate was furious because she had upset Déjà. She said to the mother,

The Anniversary Part Two

"Bitch don't get fucked up again, my cousin already got in that ass, don't make me call him back."

Déjà was lost. She couldn't wrap her mind around what was going on. She walked to her dad's office, but he was gone. Déjà collapsed in tears in the hallway. She just lay there crying and remembering all the times her mother had been less than a mother to her. Déjà thought about how they didn't have baby pictures of her and no pictures of her mother pregnant with her, but had plenty of pictures of her older brother. Déjà's dad always said they got lost in the move from the Congo, Africa to America. Then Déjà started to remember all the evil things her mother had done to her when she was younger, like tease her about being overweight or tell her she wasn't as smart as her older brother. Déjà used to think *What mother does that?* Chocolate picked Déjà up off the floor and tried to comfort her, but she was inconsolable. Déjà said right now she just wanted to get away from that house; she always hated it there.

As Déjà and Chocolate were gathering their coats and purses, they saw Soni Lynn's mother Mary and Deja's mom in what looked like a heated conversation. Mary was pointing her finger in Déjà's mom's face, telling her, "This shit ain't over." The only problem was Mary didn't even know Déjà or her mom, so what could she possibly be talking about?

Déjà noticed her dad in the corner staring at Mary like he had seen a ghost. Mary continued to threaten Déjà's mom until her husband Romello pulled her away. Déjà was confused. What the hell was going on with Soni Lynn's mom and her mom? But right now all she wanted to do was get away from that house.

Chapter Ten

The Scariest Place on Earth

The Scariest Place on Earth

Chocolate and Déjà spent the night at Déjà's house; Chocolate gave Déjà a sleeping pill to help her rest. The next morning when she woke up she heard banging, kids laughing, and Foxy barking. At first she thought she was dreaming because she never had kids at her house. She got up to see what was going on and when she got to the hallway she saw Chocolate's little cousin and friend. They were skateboarding down her stairway ramp and the dog was chasing them. *What the fuck?* she thought. *Do they want to go flying out of that big ass glass window located directly at the bottom of the steps? One slip is all it would take for them to go flying out into the street and get killed by a car.* "Stop that," Déjà screamed as she walked down the stairs. "Do y'all wanna die?" she asked them as she walked past them.

"Aw auntie, it's nothing; I'm the skate board queen," replied Chocolate's little cousin.

"What the fuck ever," replied Déjà. "You just keep yo' skate boarding ass off my staircase. I don't want you breaking my very expensive custom designed windows."

The little cousin said "Okay, okay, auntie but when I get rich it's gon' be on."

Déjà started laughing and said, "Well, when yo' little ass get rich, you can go skateboarding down yo' own staircase" and walked in the downstairs bathroom. "Damn," she said out loud, "ain't this a bitch?" She grabbed the last pad from under the bathroom counter and some clean panties from the dryer. If the video, Chagita running around killing, Otis being gay, and the falling out with her supposed mother wasn't enough, now her out of control, unpredictable, menstrual cycle had to start today of all days. After she cleaned herself up she walked to the kitchen to get her morning cup of coffee.

She saw Chocolate in the back yard sitting by the pool having her daily breakfast (a blunt and a cup of coffee). She walked in the back yard with her and noticed a huge bundle of roses--at least three dozen perfect pink roses in a beautiful vase and some balloons that said "Happy Birthday." In all the confusion she forgot today was her birthday.

Chocolate looked at her and said, "That was a hell of a birthday gift your moms gave you last night." She continued to say, "I always hated that bitch."

Déjà said, "Yeah, me too," and they both started laughing. "Who sent the beautiful flowers?" Déjà asked.

"I don't know," Chocolate replied. "I just set them out on the deck."

Déjà walked over to the flowers and smelled them first. They were beautiful. Then she read the card. It said, "Happy Birthday, My Love." She smiled and walked away. Chocolate said, "Yeah, we both knew who sent them," and they both laughed.

The flowers were from Ghost. She found Ghost in the guest room sleep. He said when he came there Chocolate let him in and told him all about what happened. He gave her a kiss on the forehead and said, "Don't trip; it's gonna be all right."

The Scariest Place on Earth

Déjà could tell he was tired so she let him sleep. That entire morning Déjà's phone kept ringing with people wanting to wish her a happy birthday. However, Déjà wasn't in the mood; hell, she had just found out her mother wasn't really her mother, her ex's crazy baby mama had tried to fight her, Lucas' stupid ass girlfriend had played that stripping video for all her parents' friends to see and to top that off she was PMSing and Chagita was going crazy--damn, could it get any worse? Chocolate pushed the bedroom door open and said, "Get up, bitch, it's your birthday. I'm going to take you to the happiest place on earth." Chocolate said, "Bitch we going to Disneyland."

Déjà was a little reluctant but Chocolate talked her into it; besides, Disneyland was Déjà's favorite since she was a little girl. She loved eating their corndogs and riding *It's a Small World.* Plus every time they went Chocolate was always running around looking for Goofy; she would be screaming, "Has anybody seen Goofy," and that was too funny to Déjà.

Lucas showed up at Déjà's house before they left. He bought her balloons and a gift card. He was heated about the situation that happened last night and told Déjà to be strong. She was born under the Chinese new year of the monkey and that meant she could transform obstacles into opportunities and that she was uncannily clever, multitalented, and had a knack for finances.

Déjà started laughing and said, "You really believe that bullshit, don't you?"

Lucas said, "Hell yeah."

Déjà looked at him and said, "You could sell ice to Eskimos."

Lucas said, "Damn right I can," and they both started laughing. Lucas rubbed his goatee and said, "Shit, with a face this fine, it really ain't no stopping me; shit, Denzel ain't got shit on me."

"Easy playa, now you going too far," Déjà said, smiling.

Lucas gave Déjà a kiss on the forehead and said, "I gotta get out of here. I got a ten hour flight to Cambodia and a twenty-four hour layover."

"Oh yeah?" Déjà said "and what are you going to do with that spare time?"

Lucas said, laughing, with his fake Cambodian accent, "Well, you know they love me long time over there," and made a pumping motion with his penis. He continued to say, "And it don't take much; they can make you holla for a dolla, and they do anything strange for some change." He said, "And I got plenty of both."

Déjà, shaking her head at Lucas, said, "You should be ashamed of yo' self, talking about yo' people like that," and laughed.

He said, "Shit, I'm American," and smiled. Lucas started walking to the door and threw his hands up in the air and shouted, "I just love me some ho's." He stomped his feet as if he was shouting for the Lord and said, "Thank you Jesus for ho's." He started laughing and walked out the door.

When they arrived at Disneyland they decided to go to Disney adventure first. Déjà was feeling a little jittery; she knew it was her PMS and the stress. She let Chocolate's cousin trick her into getting on a water ride. The cousin told her it was just a ride that floated on the water; the only thing would happen is you would get soaking wet. Déjà didn't mind; it was hot as hell that day. Normally Déjà didn't get on rides; she just walked around and ate and watched the shows. She loved the show "Fantasia" and the parade. Déjà thought, *What the hell, it's just a kid's ride.* At first the ride was slow, just wading through water with some sharp turns. Then it got faster and came to a complete stop. That day the park was crowed, so the rides were taking a little longer.

When they stopped Chocolate's cousin informed Déjà that they were entering a tunnel with a thousand foot drop to the bottom. That information sent Déjà into a full-blown anxiety attack. She unstrapped her seat belt, got up and started screaming, "I want off." Then, to make matters worse, she started jumping from boat to boat trying to get to the control room that was right before the thousand foot drop. Everybody was trying to make her sit down.

The booth controller shut the ride down and called security. He told security he had a crazy lady trying to kill herself. Security came flying from everywhere. The only thing that stopped her from trying to get in the water to the control booth was the controller's announcement that if she got in the water, she surely was going to die. Déjà stopped dead in her tracks and said, "Die? No, I know how to swim."

The controller informed her that swimming was the least of her worries. He told her that the water had mechanical equipment in it that would rip her to shreds. Déjà rethought her decision to get off, plus in her crazy

167

mind she didn't have on the right outfit to meet God and her lime green nail polish surely wasn't appropriate for Heaven. No, she thought, dying today wasn't an option. She sat in a boat next to some foreigners who where starring at her like she had lost her fucking mind.

The controller told all the people that they had to shut the ride down and evacuate its passengers one by one, which would take a while. Everybody was pointing and whispering, talking about the crazy lady who tried to jump off the ride. The little girl in front of Déjà looked at her and sarcastically said, "You scared of a kid's ride? Didn't you read the sign?" Déjà just looked at the little girl.

When they got to Déjà's boat and evacuated her, the head of security asked her if she needed a doctor or if she was on any kind of medication. Déjà replied no and that she just had an anxiety attack from stress. He advised her that normally she would be asked to leave the park but since she didn't appear to be a troublemaker that he would let her stay. He told her maybe she should stay off the rides and stick to the shows and attractions. Déjà agreed and apologized.

Chocolate checked to see if Déjà was okay before she started teasing her. All the little kids by the ride started pointing at her and whispering, "That's the crazy lady who got the ride shut down."

Déjà was so embarrassed. She and Chocolate decided to let the girls explore the park on their own. They just had to check in every hour on the cell phone. Déjà and Chocolate sat down and talked. Then they went to see the princess show and all the exhibits. The rest of the day turned out pretty good. It took Déjà's mind off her mama drama. Her nerves seemed to be calming down.

When Déjà pulled into her driveway she saw her dad's car parked outside. When she opened the door she saw her dad sitting on the patio in the dark, drinking what looked like hard liquor and eating potato chips.

Chocolate took the girls upstairs to give them some privacy. Déjà looked at her dad. Normally he was a very attractive man, but today he looked like he had been crying. He said with his thickest accent, "Baby girl, do you know that there is nothing healthy in here to eat?" Then he ate a chip. He said, "But you have an exceptional liquor cabinet," and lifted up his glass of Hennessey and drank the entire glass. He looked at Déjà while he was pouring another drink and said, "But don't drink too much; it's bad for your liver."

Déjà smiled and said, "Okay Daddy, I will remember that" as she sat in the chair next to him.

He sat back in his chair, folded his hands and closed his eyes. He said, "Baby girl, let me tell you a story." Déjà got up from her chair and sat at his feet, holding his leg like she used to when he would tell her stories when she was a little girl. He began to tell his story. He said, "Do you know what betroth means?"

Déjà answered, "Yes, it's a mutual promise to marry someone."

He said, "Yes, that's correct. Well, a long time ago when I was a young, poor teenager in the Republic of the Congo, I wanted to go to school but my family was too poor. My parents arranged for me to go to school,

169

college and medical school. They made arrangements with a very wealthy family to pay for my schooling; all I had to do was marry their youngest daughter when I graduated." He said, "This wasn't a big deal to me; families in Africa have been arranging marriages for centuries, plus their daughter wasn't bad looking. After I finished all my schooling I did just that; I married their daughter and your brother was born nine months later."

Déjà was just sitting there listening; she wasn't saying a word. She had already figured out that her daddy wasn't truly in love with her mother. Although she had never seen him with other women, she knew he had a few and it didn't help the situation that her mother screamed all the time that he was an adulterer in Swahili (when she was really pissed she spoke in Swahili).

He continued with his story. He said, "While I was working at a dentist's office in a small village with Zira's (Chocolate's real name) father, we met two beautiful African American missionaries; they would come to the village and volunteer. They were college graduates who had committed two years of their lives to the children in Africa. They both were nurses by trade but did whatever was needed." He stopped his story and looked up to see Chocolate listening in the door. He said to Chocolate, "Come, you need to hear this too." Chocolate walked over and sat on the ground next to Déjà. Chocolate held Déjà's hand as he continued to tell his story. He said, "Zira, your dad fell in love with your mother as soon as he saw her. They were married and very happy. I took notice of your mother's best friend. She was the most beautiful woman I had ever laid eyes on. She was smart, funny, outspoken--she had a spirit about her that was intoxicating. I knew I had to have her from the moment I laid eyes on her, but I was married and had a son at home. At first I kept my distance from her, until the attraction was undeniable. Although we both knew it was wrong we started seeing each other." He pressed both his lips together tightly then he said, "Even though I didn't love my wife like I loved her, I'd made a commitment to her and her family. When I explained that commitment to her she didn't get angry or upset. She just said 'I understand', and we agreed that we would end the relationship. She stopped coming to the small town. I didn't see her for months, but she was in my mind and in my heart. So I went looking for her. Zira's mother refused to tell me where she was. She begged me to let her be, but I couldn't. I went to the Red Cross looking for her and they told me she was volunteering at the hospital in Pointe-Noire, which was a few hours' drive away from the small village where I worked."

He stopped talking to hold back his tears; it seemed like telling this story was very painful for him. He rubbed Déjà's hair then he continued. By this time both girls were glued to their seats and he had their full attention. He said, "When I got there the hospital gave me the name of the hotel where she was staying. I waited in the lobby for her for hours, until she finally came home. She smiled at me when she saw me; that let me know she missed me as much as I missed her. We sat and talked in the lobby. I told her I was leaving my wife. She stopped me and said she could never allow me to do that; she said she would never steal another woman's husband. She insisted that if I was leaving my wife it wouldn't be for her." He then looked down at Déjà and said, "We argued back and forth until I got a glimpse of her stomach. She was wearing a big shirt but I could see the outline of her stomach. I placed my hand on her stomach. How many months?' I asked her. She looked me square in my eyes and said, 'About six months and before you ask, yes, she's yours.' I replied, 'A baby girl?'

She laughed and said, 'I'm not for sure but by the way I'm carrying her in my hips, I would say so.'" He laughed and said, "She was always like that with her American wives' tales. I told her there was no certain way women carried boys or girls. She insisted that her grandmother told her that if your belly is low it's a boy but if your hips spread it's a girl." He smiled; it appeared that the memory of her made him happy. Déjà had never quite seen him smile like that.

He continued his story. He said, "She was very stubborn; she refused to let me help her. She said she was a big girl and could take care of herself. I refused to listen. I insisted that she come back closer to the small village where I worked. Finally she agreed. I set her up in a small apartment and a few months later she gave birth to a beautiful baby girl whom she named Déjà Blue." Tears flowed from Déjà's eyes. He said, "She named you Déjà, short for Rio De Janerio. She said that's where she was originally supposed to do her missionary work, but at the last minute she was reassigned to Africa." He smiled and said, "Lucky me." He looked at Déjà and said, "I loved you since the first day I laid eyes on you. You were just as beautiful as your mother, a tiny little baby with big, strong lungs." He laughed and said, "To keep you from crying, your mother drove in circles around the apartment building."

Déjà said with tears in her eyes, "What happened to her? Why did she leave me with Mommy?" Déjà was still calling the woman who raised her mommy; hell, she didn't know what else to call her because for thirty years she had been her mother.

Her dad looked down at the ground and his entire facial expression changed. A look of rage came over his face. He balled his fist up and said,

The Scariest Place on Earth

"Well, I kept you and your mom a secret for a while, until one day my wife followed me to the apartment where you and your mom lived. She was outraged. She demanded I put an end to this outrageous behavior immediately. I refused. I told her I wanted a divorce and I was leaving and taking my son. As we were arguing, we were interrupted by the devastating news that Chocolate's dad, my cousin, was killed by the rebels in a drunken bar fight." He looked down at Chocolate and said, "Your dad loved you very much." He said, "After the funeral I was packing my clothes to leave when I got called to an emergency. One of the village kids had fallen and cracked all their teeth. When I came out of surgery, I went to the apartment where you and your mom were." He hesitated. Tears were streaming down his cheeks. He got up from his chair and walked over to the side of the pool to compose himself.

He said, "When I got there the apartment was a mess. It looked like somebody had broken in. I ran to the bedroom." He fell to his knees; he put his head in his hands and sobbed like a newborn baby. He said, "I found her on the bedroom floor with her face cut up and her throat sliced from ear to ear. She was dead. I picked her up off the floor and laid her on the bed. I was scared to look any further. I searched the entire apartment for you, until I found you in the closet in the dirty clothes hamper with tape on your mouth. I didn't know what to do. I called the police and they said it had to have been a rebel killing, but I knew better. Besides, the rebels would have never touched your mother. I had an understanding with the rebel commander that nobody in my family would ever be touched."

He continued to say that he had saved the rebel captain's life by treating an abscess he had on his tooth. He removed the tooth and started giving the rebel captain treatments for his teeth. He said the rebel captain was so

173

grateful to be out of pain that he promised to protect him and his family. He started sending all the rebels to get their teeth fixed; hell, he himself had braces put on his teeth. Chocolate's dad's death was an accident. He got drunk and started a fight at the bar. One of the rebels hit him and he fell and hit his head, causing a fatal blow. He said, "But that was something they would never do, especially the cutting of the throat and face--that was personal."

He said that if the rebels had killed her, they would have raped and brutalized her first and that she was neither raped nor brutalized. He said he was lost; he didn't know what to do. He said the only woman he had ever loved was gone and his daughter was left without a mother and a home. He sat back down in the chair. He lit up a cigarette and poured another drink. He said, "I took you to Chocolate's mother for safekeeping. I didn't tell her what I had suspected; she had just lost her husband and best friend. Then I went to see the real killer. I knew in my heart my wife had done this. When I got to the house she was pretending she had just come from the market. When I asked her about what happened, what she said infuriated me she replied, 'I know nothing of the death of your whore, but I don't feel sorry for your whore; she got what she deserved.' In my rage I grabbed her by her throat and dug my thumb into her windpipe. I would have killed her if it wasn't for your brother screaming, 'Don't kill mommy.' Your brother ran out of the house. I didn't go after him. I stayed to confront my wife who had become this devil bitch. The hate in her eyes was heartbreaking. My rejection of her had turned her into a monster. The guilt over what I had done to her was overwhelming. My love for another woman had driven her crazy enough to murder another human being. So much shame filled my heart. I simply walked away from her. I didn't even listen to her lies. I went out to find my son. I found him crying in the back seat of his mother's car, holding the same tape I found over your mouth."

He looked down at Déjà and said, "My six year old son was holding the same tape that I had just found on my baby girl's mouth." He said, "Imagine my pain and confusion. I asked your brother where he got it from. He said, 'From mommy's car earlier.' He was shaking with fear. He said, 'Is mommy going to kill us too, like she did the lady?' My heart broke into tiny pieces. My son had witnessed his mother killing his sister's mother. I put him in my lap and told him to tell me what happened.

"He said his mother was crying and drinking wine all day, then she put him in the car and drove to the apartment. He said his mother told him to stay in the car until she came back but he didn't listen; he sneaked out of the car and followed her into the apartment. He said you were asleep in the other room. When you heard the shouting you woke up crying. He said they didn't hear you because they were shouting so loud. He said you wouldn't stop crying so he put the tape he had been playing with in the car over your mouth to shut you up. Your brother said you were too little to remove it. He said he then saw his mother grab the lady and cut her face and slash her throat. He said he was horrified and ran and hid in the closet, and he stuck you in the dirty clothes hamper to keep his mom from finding you. He said she searched the apartment for the baby but got scared when the phone rang and ran out the door. He said he then ran out the back door, so it just looked like he had wandered off. He said she drove home, burned her bloody clothes and took a shower. She asked him why he got out of the car he told her that he saw a dog and was chasing it."

Déjà asked, "So my brother knew all these years Mommy wasn't really my mommy?"

"Yes," her dad replied, "Yes, he knew. I made him promise to never tell you." He said, "It still haunts him to this day; however, she doesn't know that he knows."

Déjà was furious with her Dad. She said, "Why would you allow that women to raise me if you knew what she was capable of, and why isn't she in jail, anyway?"

Déjà's dad replied "When I calmed your brother down and assured him that his mother wasn't going to kill him too, I walked back to the house. I had made a decision not to call the police and have my wife and the mother of my son arrested, but I was leaving and taking my son." He looked at Déjà and said, "I know that's hard for you to understand; however, I felt it was my fault. I had driven her mad with my lies and deceit. When I entered the kitchen I found her lying in a puddle of blood on the floor. She had slit both her wrists."

He got up walked around for a few seconds. He began again, "Can you imagine my situation? My lover was dead, my cousin was dead, my son was in fear of his life, my baby girl was alone without a mother, and my wife was lying on the floor bleeding to death. I knew I couldn't have taken her to the hospital; for God's sake, she was a respected Doctor. That would have surely been the end of her career. I rushed her to the clinic where I worked, stitched her wrists together and gave her a blood transfusion. When she awakened she was different, as if she didn't know what was going on or what had happened. She was losing her mind. I had to watch her twenty-four hours. Between watching her and checking on you and your bother, I was beginning to think I was going to lose my mind. Finally she started getting better. She started to remember and she was riddled with grief over what she had done. She begged for my forgiveness and said she suffered a moment of insanity."

He laid his head back in the chair and said, "She was my wife, my son needed a mother and I felt she was truly sorry. After a few months we decided to move to America to get away from what had happened. The plan was Chocolate's mother would take you and raise you, and when you were old enough to understand, I was going to explain to you about your mother. However, it didn't go as planned. Chocolate's mother got hooked on drugs to ease her pain and I had to take you." He said, "I forced my wife to accept you and she resented me for it. I think in my own way I was punishing her for what she had done. And the fact that you looked exactly like your mother made the situation worse. Every day she had to see you as a reminder of my infidelity."

Déjà took a deep breath and said, "What did she look like?"

Her dad reached in his wallet and took out an old picture that he had restored to its original likeness. He said, "This is her" and handed the picture to Déjà.

Déjà was scared to look at the picture. She slowly looked down and saw the spitting image of her. Tears rolled down her face as she studied her mom's picture she said, "What was her name?"

He smiled as he looked at the picture with Déjà. He said, "Charlene. Her name was Charlene, and I loved her with all my heart." He told Déjà she could have the picture but Déjà could see how much that picture meant to her father and she could feel the pain talking about her caused him.

She said, "No Daddy, you keep it. I know it means a lot to you. How about you make me a copy?"

He smiled at her and put the picture back in his wallet. He said, "I've had this picture for over thirty years; it means the world to me."

Déjà saw that this conversation had drained her father, so she suggested he lie down in her room. He hugged her and Chocolate and walked away slowly. He stopped at the door with his back to them and his head down and said, "I love both of you more than you guys could ever know. Both of you are reminders of the two people I loved most in this world--never forget that." Then he said, "Oh yeah, baby girl, it is not okay for you to be stripping! Stay off the pole."

Chapter Eleven

The Beat Down

The Beat Down

If that little tramp bitch thinks for one fucking second she's going to get away with that bullshit she pulled last night, that bitch better think again, Déjà thought to herself. Déjà got up at 4:30am, put on her leather black Chuck Taylor's, her black gloves with the fingers cut out and grabbed her Louisville slugger. As she was walking out the door she saw Chocolate standing by her car. "You not going," Déjà said as she hit the alarm to the car.

"The hell if I ain't," replied Chocolate. "I'll be damned if I'm going to let my cousin roll up in Inglewood on some bitch alone."

Déjà looked at Chocolate with that "I'm not motherfucking playing" look. Then Chocolate said, "Besides, I'm just going to be there for backup; you know them ho's are scandalous!" Then she tapped her backpack where she kept a plethora of weapons including but not limited to her favorite Saturday night special.

Déjà knew Chocolate was just going to follow her if she left her. Déjà frowned at Chocolate and said, "Get in bitch, but I got this."

Chocolate lit up her breakfast (a blunt), blew out some smoke, and said, "And I got you!"

When they pulled up to the house where the stripper lived it was quiet. The sun was just coming up. Déjà grabbed her Louisville slugger and proceeded to the door with Chocolate right behind her on her heels. Déjà knocked on the door and waited. Déjà was still heated about that video the stripper played at her parents' anniversary party. "Who is it?" Déjà heard a voice from the other side of the door.

181

The Beat Down

"UPS," Déjà replied. As soon as the door opened and Déjà saw the stripper's face she stole on her right in the eye. When the girl hit the floor Déjà jumped on her and started beating her in the face with her fist. The stripper tried to fight back but Déjà was too much for her. Déjà was bigger and stronger, plus Déjà was enraged at what she had done.

"What the fuck is going on?" said the stripper's big beastly friend running toward them from the back of the house.

Chocolate pulled out her .45 pistol and drew down on her. Chocolate said, "Hold up, this ain't got shit to do with you. It's between them, now back down."

The girl put her hands up in the air and said, "Who the fuck is you? That's my homegirl," and pointed to the stripper.

Chocolate said, "Again, this ain't got shit to do with you. Who I am is irrelevant, but for the record, the bitch whooping the shit out of your homegirl is my cousin."

The girl just stood there with her hands in the air. She said, "This is some bullshit."

Déjà was beating the shit out of the stripper until she was out of breath. Déjà, barely able to breathe, kicked the stripper in the side then said, "Bitch stay out of my business and mind your own." Déjà put her hands on her knees and took in some deep breaths. The stripper was lying on the floor bleeding. When Déjà caught her breath she looked over at Chocolate holding her .45 pistol on the stripper's friend. Then she looked around the house. "What the fuck is going on in here?" said Déjà as she looked at what looked like stolen electrical equipment, name brand purses, jewelry, blank checkbooks, and credit cards.

Chocolate said, "Look like somebody got sticky fingers and some skills working with stolen credit cards and checks."

Déjà looked over at the stripper, who was now leaning against the wall, and said, "Stupid bitch, you got all this going on and still got time to fuck with me? You one ignorant bitch."

"Fuck you," the stripper replied.

Déjà just smiled at her and said, "You ain't never going to learn."

Chocolate looked at Déjà and said, "Let's bounce." The big beastly girl was looking like she had something to say. Chocolate, pointing her pistol at her, said, "Once again, this is between them two. I ain't got no issues with you, and you most definitely don't want to have a problem with me!"

The girl looked Chocolate up and down, then shook Chocolate's hand and said, "We cool." Then she handed Chocolate and Déjà two name brand handbags. She said, "And y'all ain't seen none of this."

Déjà said, "We ain't seen nothing!" Then she and Chocolate walked out the door and drove off! When they got back to the house Déjà checked herself for scratches and bruises. She found none. Monday morning as she drove to work she looked at the handbags the big beastly girl had given her and Chocolate. Both handbags at first glance looked to be worth a few thousand. Déjà thought to herself that all the rumors about somebody stealing the customer's credit cards down at the Wet Kitty were true. Damn, Déjà thought, this stupid ass stripper was committing credit card fraud and had a house full of stolen property but still had time to be concerned about her. Déjà thought, *She is as dumb as they come.*

Before she entered the building she thought she'd drop by the child care first to check on her little killer Chagita. Damn, Déjà thought to herself, she was surrounded by criminals. She found Chagita sitting at her desk, gathering her thoughts. Déjà said, "Hey lady bug what's good?"

Chagita looked up and frowned when she spied state licensing walking through the front door. "Fuck," Chagita said out loud, despite the three year old sitting in her office 'cause he couldn't help himself from biting the shit out of his classmates. Chagita told Déjà she was not in the mood to deal with this dike ass lady today.

Déjà started laughing and said, "I'll stay with you."

From the looks of it, the state licensing lady was in full dike mode that day. For starters, she had her motorcycle helmet in her hands, along with her black riding gloves. She was wearing a plaid button down shirt, utility pants and for some reason unbeknownst to Chagita and Déjà she had cut all her hair off to a short spiky mess. But her black Harley Davison cowboy boots stole the show. Chagita just rolled her eyes to herself as she stood in awe of the horrific sight she was seeing. She couldn't believe state licensing would allow her to wear that to work, looking like a lesbian lumber jack. As the lady made her way toward them, Chagita looked down at the little biter sitting in her office. She said, "Do one thing and you

The Beat Down

gonna be on timeout until Jesus come back, understand?"

He looked at her and nodded his head yes. From the look in his eyes, Déjà knew he knew Chagita was crazy. And although he didn't know who Jesus was or where he went, he did know that if he showed out he was going to be sitting in that chair until he came back.

The lady walked over and introduced herself as if her ass had never been there before. "Hello, I'm Andrea Black. I'm from state licensing. I'm here to inspect your facility. Who's in charge?"

Chagita just assumed she was acting stank because last year when she was there she flirted shamelessly with Chagita. When Chagita appeared to be uninterested she cited the preschool for using the bathroom as a storage room. Chagita shook her hand and replied, "Yes, I'm Santiaga. I'm the director."

They proceeded to tour the facility. Chagita wasn't worried about passing the inspection; she ran a tight ship. She was, however, a little nervous about opening up a new "mildly ill program"--that was territory she had never been in. But she figured it would help all the sick children who truly wanted to attend school and whose parents had to go to work. They made their way through the facility, and everything seemed to be going well… until the licensing lady decided to bend down at eye level to the little biter, who had accompanied them the entire tour without incident.

She said, "Hey little fella, do you like coming here?" He stood there looking at her as if he thought she was stupid. He said nothing. Then she said, "What's your name? My name is Ms. Andrea. "She patted his head with her hand. "Such a cute little fella," she said.

Chagita stood next to them and started to tell her his name, but before she could get it out he grabbed hold of Andrea and bit the living shit out of her hand. For some reason he wouldn't let go. Chagita had to pry her hand from his mouth. Finally he let her hand go, then he burst into tears and took off running down the hall toward the door. Chagita took off running after him. When she caught him, he was out of breath and threw himself to the ground. She had one of the teachers who happened to be on her break get him and take him to another room. Then she insisted that Déjà deal with it. Hell, Chagita figured Déjà was way better suited to handle this situation than her.

Chagita calmly walked over to Andrea. She didn't know what to say. She stood there for a second, staring at the teeth-prints in Andrea's flesh. She thought to herself, *Damn, that had to hurt.* They escorted her to her office and took out the first aid kit. *Shit,* she thought to herself, *now this heffa is going to try to cite the facility for some petty reason.* Chagita gently took her hand and wiped it with antibiotic rinse. As she was rinsing her hand she noticed it made Andrea uneasy. Chagita looked up at Déjà and then to the sky and whispered, "Lord, forgive me." Then she slowly massaged Andrea's hand. Hell, she figured that if Andrea was getting such a thrill out of her touching her hand then that would persuade Andrea not to be such a bitch and not cite them. It seemed to be working; as she enjoyed the massage to her hand; she said; "Oh, don't worry about it; kids will be kids. Besides, with a caring, nurturing woman like you, he is in the best hands." Then she gave Chagita this look as if she was undressing her with her eyes.

The Beat Down

Finally Déjà spoke up. She said, "Excuse me, am I interrupting something?" Then she frowned at Chagita.

Andrea snatched her hand from Chagita and said, "Oh no, no, it's just another exciting day in the life of a preschool." She held up her hand so Déjà could see her bite. "He has a pretty strong set of choppers; somebody's been drinking lots of milk." All the women gave this fake laugh.

Andrea left her report with Chagita and bid the ladies a good afternoon. Chagita & Déjà watched Andrea leave.

When she was out of sight Déjà turned to Chagita and said, "Okay, please tell me what the hell happened and what the hell y'all got going, and please don't tell me you crossing over because by the way you was stroking MamaDoo's hand, I would have to question what team you was really on." They both started cracking up laughing. "Bitch, you going straight to hell for that; got that heffa all steamed up."

Both ladies were laughing so hard they were doubled over holding their stomachs and tears were rolling down their faces. When the teacher came in and told them that the little boy said he bit her because her hair looked like Chucky, they both fell on the floor screaming with laughter.

As Déjà was walking out wiping her tears from laughing, she turned to Chagita and said, "Ok chick, I'm gone. Anything else you wanna tell me about this school before I leave?"

Chagita looked at her with this silly, suspicious look. "Nope, not one thing," she replied.

Déjà just shook her head; she knew by the way Chagita said it something was wrong. Déjà looked at her and said, "Is it a full-blown disaster yet?"

Chagita looked guilty and sat down at her desk. She replied, "Nope, not a hurricane, just a strong storm, but I can handle it. Don't worry, I got this."

Déjà shook her head as she walked away, "Ok, ok, but don't come to me later saying you misjudged it and it's really a category four hurricane. As a matter of fact, let me hear what's going on." Déjà turned back around and sat down.

Chagita pulled a file from her file cabinet. "Bitch," she mumbled and smacked her lips as she read the papers in the file. One of the parents at the school was threatening to file a lawsuit against the school for violating her child's civil rights. Chagita felt it was bullshit. It all started when one of the teachers refused to let the parent's son wear a princess costume for Halloween. Then it escalated when the same teacher refused to let the little boy wear girls' clothes to school. The parent was furious and said the teacher was stifling her child's development. She insisted that he had the right to express who he was. She said that he enjoyed dressing up in girls' clothes and that it was a part of who he was. She was adamant about allowing him the freedom to be who he was. The teacher refused to allow such behavior, not because she didn't want him to express himself, but because when he wore girls' clothing all the children laughed and teased him. He didn't care, but it interrupted the classroom. And to make matters worse, when the parent came to complain to Chagita, she made the mistake of referring to the child's mom as his grandmother. "Hell,"

The Beat Down

Chagita told Déjà, "she is in her early fifties--a little old to be having a four year old." The parent was furious when Chagita refused to allow her boy child to wear girls' clothes. This is how the lawsuit came about.

Chagita explained to Déjà she found a way to get around the lawsuit. She decided that the entire preschool had to wear uniforms. That way if he wanted to wear a dress, at least it wouldn't be adorned with rhinestones and sparkles. Everybody was going to have to wear white and navy blue uniforms. Chagita sat down at her desk. She was trying to figure out how in hell this mother could allow such foolishness. Chagita told Déjà one good ass whooping and he would gladly decide to dress like a boy. "What the fuck," she said, "that's what's wrong with these children today--too much freedom."

Déjà just sat there laughing. Déjà thought it was ridiculous that this mother would even suggest that Chagita was trying to violate her four year old's civil rights and his choice to dress like a little girl. Déjà looked at Chagita and said, "Damn, she proud her son's a little fag?"

They both started cracking up laughing again! Chagita said, "You better not dare let your secretary hear you say that."

Déjà pulled herself together and said, "Girl, that fool would be down here every day giving him fashion tips," then they started laughing again. Déjà started for the door. She said, "Make sure you give the parents plenty time to get these uniforms, and if that little diva comes with a uniform dress on, as long as he pays his tuition, so be it."

Chagita frowned and started laughing. She said, "Oh yeah, I'm riding with

The Beat Down

Luscious and her producer friend to San Diego this weekend. John Paul is going to meet us there for dinner, and I may fly back to Mexico with him for a few days."

Déjà thought to herself that Chagita must be really taken with John Paul, and Luscious was gone over this producer. She said, "That's nice, ladybug. Have fun and don't kill nobody." Déjà gave her a hug and went up to her office.

Her secretary was fussing about some strange white man coming to look for Déjà and touching all the stuff on his desk. He had the Lysol out, wiping his desk down. He looked at Déjà and said, "He didn't look that friendly, either." Déjà asked if he had an accent and the secretary said, "Yeah, sounded Russian."

Déjà was happy for her two friends, Luscious and Chagita; however, she was still concerned about Chocolate, even though Chocolate said she was cool with her situation with Otis, but she still hadn't heard from him and every time she contacted the prison they informed her that he'd taken her off his visiting list and that they couldn't release any personal information to her, even though she was his wife. They said only his lawyer was privy to that information. Déjà decided to stop by Chocolate's tattoo shop and check on her, but first she was going to check on Luscious because Luscious didn't look like she was feeling well after the party. Every now and then her heart gave her problems and her swinging around that pole at the Wet Kitty didn't help it none.

As Déjà approached the tattoo shop she felt like somebody was watching her. She just shook it off as bad nerves due to her current situation; shit, there was a lot going on. Plus she and Chocolate had to get that bag of money out of her garage. She called Ghost before she went in the tattoo shop. During the conversation she got an alert from social media telling her she had a message from Lucas. He was still in Cambodia. Déjà just figured his cheap ass didn't want to pay the international fees. She decided to check it later.

Chocolate was in her office doing some paperwork. Déjà knew she was just trying to keep herself busy to distract her from thinking about Otis. "How you holding up, girlie?" Déjà asked Chocolate as she sat down. Déjà put her purse on the table.

"Is that the purse that bitch gave us?" Chocolate asked Déjà.

"Yep, I know I'm pitiful but shit, it's nice," Déjà replied, and they both started laughing. Déjà knew Chocolate was never going to come and pick up her purse, so she'd be carrying hers next week. Chocolate just wasn't into girly stuff--never had been. She preferred guns. "So girlie, what are you going to do about Otis?"

Chocolate just put her head down and replied, "It's nothing I can do if he doesn't want to talk to me. Shit, I guess just wait for the divorce papers."

The room got sort of silent after that comment. Déjà thought she'd use some psychology 101 on her. She said, "So how do you feel about that, Chocolate?"

Chocolate just looked at her at first with a blank stare, like she was confused about the question. Then she replied, "Bitch, how do you think I feel about this shit? It's fucked up! This motherfucker I've devoted half my life to, had a child for, and kept my promise to him to do my part in our marriage–and all of a sudden I find out he's gay, fucking his cell mate, and wants a divorce. Bitch, I just feel great," she said sarcastically. Then she continued to say, "Shit, I have so many questions, like when did he realize he was gay, how many niggas he been fucking, was he using protection when he was ramming these niggas in the ass--shit, the list of questions just goes on and on." She was silent for a second she said, "I had an HIV test the other day. I'm waiting on the results."

Now Déjà had the blank stare of confusion. She thought to herself, *Hell, maybe Psychology 101 wasn't the right way to go.* Déjà said, "I'm sure you will be fine and until I hear Otis tell me out of his mouth that he likes fucking men, I'm not going to believe a word." Déjà told Chocolate that she was going to have a lawyer friend of Soni Lynn's check into the situation, because if nothing else, Otis owed her an explanation and a apology face to face. Déjà was getting mad seeing her cousin so hurt.

Chocolate said in a somber tone, "You know he was my first."

Déjà laughed and said, "Girl, don't talk about first; you know that was a horrific experience for me."

Chocolate laughed until she cried remembering Déjà's first. Chocolate said, "Bitch, you the only heffa I know who wants to go to the emergency room after their first time, talking about you may be bleeding to death."

Déjà had to laugh. She said, "Shit, you told me he was going to go inside me; you never said he was going to go in and out."

The Beat Down

When Déjà said that, Chocolate fell on the floor laughing. She said, "Oh my God, bitch, you need help. Sometimes I wonder if you hear the shit you say!" They both started cracking up laughing. Chocolate said, "Bitch, we had to let you soak in the tub for hours. I was so happy when yo' ass fell asleep. Then you woke up still tripping."

Déjà and Chocolate laughed until both were out of breath. After their visit Chocolate seemed to be feeling better. They went to Déjà's house to get the bag of cash out of the garage. They didn't know what the hell they were going to do about this Russian dude. Déjà decided to call The Chief about the situation because it seemed to be serious. She wasn't sure if he would even get involved, but he was their only choice. After they got the bag of cash from the garage and hid it in the crawl space under the house, Déjà got a phone call from Chagita telling her that Luscious and her boyfriend were involved in a terrible accident in Tijuana.

Déjà said, "What the hell was they doing in Tijuana? You said y'all was going to San Diego?"

Chagita explained that they did go to San Diego but decided to drive to Tijuana to drink, and when they got there Luscious got drunk and started complaining of chest pains. When she blacked out they rushed her to the hospital. There were no street lights on the road they were on and they had a head-on collision. Luscious' boyfriend was ejected from the car flew, through the windshield and was in critical condition. She said she was in the back seat and suffered a broken arm and leg. However, during the accident Luscious Had a massive heart attack and was still unconscious. Déjà was floored; this shit couldn't be happening.

Chapter Twelve

Blue Eyes

Blue Eyes

Déjà, her daddy, Chocolate, and Chocolate's skateboarding niece were all having hamburgers and chili cheese fries for dinner, courtesy of Déjà's dad. He loved junk food every now and then and since he wasn't allowed to eat it at home, he gorged on it at Déjà's house. They heard the bell ring. Déjà just knew it was Ghost; she heard his loud ass motorcycle before the doorbell rang. She knew that the guard had just let him in because he had sweet talked her, too. He always flirted with the security and they loved it. To Déjà's surprise and displeasure, it was her so-called mom. Déjà stood there at first, just taking in this outfit she had on: all black studded leather jacket with zippers, leather pants, thigh high black studded leather riding boots and holding a hot pink helmet. *What the fuck?* Déjà thought. *This bitch is truly losing it.* She did have to admit the boots and jacket were hot, but the leather pants and hot pink helmet were a little much.

She looked Déjà up and down with that "bitch I can't stand you" look and said, "Tell your father to come to the door. I got a surprise for him."

Déjà replied, "Shit, you got more surprises? Seems like after that smack-down you got after your last surprise, you would be done with that," then she returned the same "bitch I can't stand you" look and screamed for her dad.

He came to the door and said, "Get the hell out of here. Nobody wants you here, be gone."

She smiled that evil, sneaky, devilish smile she had when she knew his guilt over his past actions leading her to kill would bring him home. She said, "Aw, don't be like that. I've come to apologize and give you your anniversary gift." Then she turned around and pointed to the driveway. In the driveway was a brand new Harley with all the bells and whistles a motorcycle could have. And on the seat were a Harley jacket, helmet, and boots.

Déjà just rolled her eyes and tooted up her lips. "I know you not silly enough to think that a motorcycle is gonna be enough to forgive you for all your bullshit. The only thing that would make up for your shit would be a straitjacket and a padded cell."

"Hell naw," Chocolate added in her two cents, "naw, a single bullet to the head would be better."

"Now ladies, that's no way for such beautiful creatures to be talking." They looked around to see where the strange voice came from.

Déjà's mom looked like she had just heard the devil himself. She was frozen with fear. Déjà's dad grabbed Déjà and tried to pull her back into the house, but it was too late. They saw two men come from nowhere, and two men were already in the house. Déjà's dad looked at the two men standing in front of them. One was holding a huge gun and the other had his hoisted (Déjà could see the outline under his suit jacket). Chocolate recognized one of the men. He was the same Russian creep that held her in the motel room. The other man she had never seen. From the way Déjà's dad and mom were staring at him, she had a feeling they both recognized him and they both feared him. He stood in front of Déjà's mom and kissed her on the cheek. "My dearest sister, looking quite the little adventuress, I might say. I don't think I've ever seen this look on you; spicing it up, are you?"

Blue Eyes

Déjà's mom didn't say a word. It looked like she was going to shit in her pants. He ordered everyone in the house. He told the other men to tie them up and sit them on the sofa. He told them to make the ropes on Déjà's father, who he referred to as the "Mandingo Warrior", extra tight; seemed like he loathed Déjà's father. He pulled up a chair and sat down. Déjà got a good look at him. He was medium height, medium build, dark brown, and from the markings on his face and his accent Déjà knew he was from Africa, because her dad had the same markings. From what Déjà could see of his face, he was very attractive, and the slight touches of grey hair around his edges Déjà found to be quite sexy. He had shades on, which Déjà found to be odd since it was nighttime. He walked over to Déjà and ordered her to stand up.

Déjà's dad screamed, "Stay away from her, monster."

He stopped in his tracks. He made a "tic tic tic" sound with his teeth. He said, "Now Solomon, is that any way to talk to your best friend slash brother-in–law? All the years you've known me, all the time we've spent together and this is your opinion of me--monster? Well, I could say the same about you and add a few more things to it, such as killer, liar, hypocrite, adulterer, woman stealer, and the list could go on and on, but I'll stop there for now. Let's start with this new name you've given yourself, Rashard! What kind of name is that? Sounds like some homosexual bartender's name." Then he gave a devilish grin and said, "I always questioned what team you were batting for." He laughed and shook his head. "I can tell by the look of confusion on dearest Déjà's face she's confused. Well, Little One," he said, looking at Déjà, "let me enlighten you about your dearest dad Solomon!"

Blue Eyes

Then he looked over at Déjà's dad and said, "Oh what a tangled web we weave when we at first set out to deceive." He sat back in the chair, crossed his legs, took a deep breath, leaned his head over to the side to get a better look at Déjà, and slowly took off his thousand dollar pair of sunglasses. Déjà knew they were a thousand bucks because she'd wanted some herself. To Déjà's surprise he was extremely handsome, with the bluest eyes she'd ever seen. It was kind of odd; she'd never seen an African man with crystal blue eyes. It was sort of scary and sexy at the same time. She knew this wasn't a good time or place but *Damn, he's fine,* she thought to herself.

He looked at Déjà, pointed to his eyes, and said, "Genetic defect--only one in a million pure blood Africans are born with blue eyes. Go figure; I had to be that one. All my life they've been a curse. When I was a young child the kids in my tribe were afraid of me. They called me 'the monster'; the ones who weren't afraid of me teased and taunted me relentlessly, to the point my parents sent me away to boarding school in Europe. However, there was one boy from my town who wasn't afraid of me. He even befriended me and took up for me." Then he looked over at Déjà's dad. "My time spent in Europe was used constructively I learned several languages, earned three degrees, and traveled to meet all sorts of fascinating individuals, such as my associate next to me. Then he pointed to the Russian that had held Chocolate hostage and tried to rape her and dope her up.

Déjà spoke up. "Well then you must be a monster, because birds of a feather flock together, and your so-called associate terrorized my cousin and killed my dog."

This information displeased him; Déjà could tell by his demeanor. He got up and walked toward her, then the Russian said, as if he was scared, "She's a damn liar."

The man put his hand in the air to silence the Russian. "Tell me, Little One, why would you say such a horrible thing against my associate?"

Then Chocolate spoke up and told the story of how he held her hostage in the hotel room with the other Russian lady and how they both escaped. This information outraged him. He pulled his gun out and put it at the temple of his associate's head. Déjà noticed it had a silencer on it. She knew a lot about guns thanks to Chocolate's fascination with them.

He asked Déjà, "Is this the truth?"

Déjà replied, "Yes, he's a psychopath."

He pulled the trigger and the Russian fell to the floor. "This is what I would do to anyone who caused you harm." He motioned to his other associates to remove the body. They dragged it to the kitchen. Everybody was frozen with fear except Déjà's father. He sat back in his chair and said, "He was only supposed to follow you, gather information, and report back; he was never to approach you."

Solomon looked at the man and blurted out, "What the hell do you want, Amir? There is nothing here for you."

He looked at Déjà's father and said, "Oh, but Solomon, there is so much here for me. I'll start with my bag and work my way down."

Déjà looked over at Chocolate; she knew exactly what bag he was referring to. Amir caught the glance she gave Chocolate. So did Solomon.

Solomon looked at Déjà and said, "Baby girl, whatever you do, don't give him the bag. Once he gets the bag he'll kill all of us."

Déjà looked at Amir staring at her as if he was amazed at her very existence. She could tell he was taken with her, but not in a way that most men are. He wasn't lusting for her; it seemed like he was longing for her friendship. She said to him, "Why would you have me and my cousin followed and why would he report back to you? Who are you?" Shit, Déjà didn't know what the hell was going on; she had just found out that her mother wasn't really her mother and her dad's name wasn't really what he said it was. Hell, what else could go wrong? "Oh yeah, and why do you keep referring to me as Little One? Do I look little to you?"

He clapped his hands together and tapped his feet. He smiled the prettiest, biggest smile. He sat back down and said "Yes, you are surely your mother's daughter: beautiful, intelligent, and hot tempered. Yes, just like your mother."

Déjà said rudely, "I'm nothing like your psycho sister and for the record, she's not my mother; your crazy sis-"

Déjà was interrupted by her father blurting out, "Enough, baby girl, don't even talk to him; he's only trouble."

Amir smiled and said, "Oh yeah, I witnessed that tragic event at your parents' anniversary party--such a fascinating event. The drunken white lady, the video of you stripping and the smack-down Solomon gave to my sister I found to be quite amusing. Oh, but Little One, I'm not talking about your fake mom," and he looked at his sister and back at Déjà. He said, "What is that name you refer to her as? Oh yeah, 'the wicked witch of Baldwin hills.'" Then he gave a little smile, "No, no, no, Little One, not her. I'm referring to your real mother, Charlene."

Déjà's dad flew into a rage at the very mention of her name. "Don't speak of her," he shouted at Amir.

"Oh Solomon, you always hated the fact that she loved me," Amir replied. Déjà eyes were wide with curiosity. She wondered what sort of relationship her real mom had with Amir and why the very mention of her name sent her father into an uproar. Amir seemed to get pleasure from Solomon's pain. "One more outburst from you, Mandingo, and you will be gagged," Amir said. "Now, Little One, let me properly introduce myself. I'm Amir Ahmad, brother to the wicked witch of Baldwin hills and friend, brother-in-law, and co-worker to the Mandingo Warrior known as Solomon. Years ago, when your father and I were colleagues we met two young, beautiful nurses from America." He looked over at Chocolate and said, "Yes Zira, I knew both your parents--such lovely people, and your dad loved you very much. Your dad was a very good loyal friend of mine, unlike Solomon." Chocolate just looked; she didn't say a word. He continued, "Right away, I was taken with her. I asked her out for coffee; she refused me at first but eventually she agreed. We developed a friendship of love and respect for each other. She even gave me a nickname she called me "Blue Eyes."

Déjà thought to herself, *Wow, what a coincidence,* because that what she called Luscious' friend. He continued his tale. They'd become the best of friends. That is, until the Mandingo Warrior (pointing to Déjà's father) ruined her. He slapped Déjà's father across the face with his gun. He started shouting, "She was perfect in every way, pure and innocent, and you violated her. You selfish bastard, you had a beautiful wife and a perfect son, but no, that wasn't enough; you seduced her with your sob stories of how you had a wounded heart and was stuck in a loveless marriage garbage. You ruined her, took advantage of her, and when you had your way with her and knocked her up, you threw her out like garbage. But I was there to pick up the pieces. I put her in a penthouse suite and promised to take care of her and her baby! And what did your sorry ass do? When you missed your toy, you came to reclaim it, just like the selfish bastard you are."

Déjà's dad screamed out, "That's a lie; she never loved you."

Amir smacked him with the gun again and ordered him gagged. Amir looked at Déjà's father bleeding from his wounds and said, "Oh, but she did love me enough to name your precious bundle of joy after me, Déjà Blue, and you hated it but she refused to change it." He looked at Déjà. "She brought you often to see me. You were the prettiest little thing she called you 'Little One'; that's why I call you that. She loved you oh so very much."

Déjà's mind was spinning with questions and doubts about her entire life. Just the other day she found out her mom wasn't her mom, she just found out her dad wasn't who he claimed to be, her real mother was murdered by her fake mother, the chief was acting like a goodie two shoes little bitch, Chagita was a killer, Luscious and Chagita were in a car crash, and now this gorgeous psychopath had them tied up, reliving his past and demanding his bag of money. Déjà thought to herself that it seemed odd that he was so pressed about that money. Déjà and Chocolate had just counted it and it was close to a few hundred thousand. But Déjà's instincts told her that he wanted something more important than money. Hell, from the looks of it, his suit cost that much. Plus her dad kept insisting that he was a killer and as soon as he got the bag he was going to take them out. Déjà wasn't so sure about that; he seemed attached to her. Déjà thought, *Oh my God, what else aren't they telling me?*

Déjà looked at Amir and said, "Are you going to tell me that Rashard-- whom you keep referring to as Solomon the Mandingo Warrior--is not my real father and that you are? You keep going on and on about how you loved my real mom." She said, "I mean, just tell me and get it over with, because my best friends are in Mexico and I really need to get to them." After Déjà told Amir what happened to them, he snapped his fingers at his associates then whispered in one's ear.

"Really?" Déjà said. "Now who's keeping secrets?"

Amir smiled and said, "Little One, I was simply telling him to get me an update on your friends' situation."

Déjà looked at Chocolate and said, "This is some bullshit--so many secrets in this dysfunctional family." She put her head down.

"Yes, yes, yes, Little One, your parents have kept many secrets from you, so let me be the one to bring you up to speed on all the deception," Amir said as he pulled out his Blackberry cell phone. He looked at Déjà and said, "Did you know that your and Chocolate's mortgages were held by the same company?"

Déjà frowned and said, "What does that have to do with anything?"

Amir smiled as he stood up and said, "Really nothing, but I'd thought you'd be interested to know that the Mandingo Warrior," he paused and glanced over at Déjà's father, "owns that company."

Déjà and Chocolate looked at each other. Déjà said, "My dad is a dentist; he doesn't own a bank;"

Amir said, "You are sadly mistaken, and I never said a bank held the mortgages to your homes." Amir sat next to Déjà and showed her some documents he pulled up on his Blackberry. He said, "Little One, you really don't know your dad at all. Your dad is so much more than this dentist. Every since we were children he wanted to be a dentist." Amir said that like he was disgusted. "Why he wanted to be a dentist was beyond me," Amir continued. "He had such a brilliant mind and steady hands." Amir removed the gag from Solomon's mouth. Déjà's dad begged with Amir to stop this foolishness or he was going to be sorry. Amir stood in front of Déjà's father and said, "Sorry how? Dead sorry? You going to blow me up too?"

Déjà's father was enraged. He started shouting how Amir was going to pay for this. Amir re-gagged him and smiled.

He looked at Déjà and said, "You know, your dad has many talents. One of them is he could build a bomb blindfolded. Did he tell you that he built and sold bombs to the highest bidders? Did he tell you that he made a deal with the US government to rat me out and save his sorry ass?" He said, "Well, let me tell you. The Mandingo Warrior made bombs of all sizes and shapes. Any kind of explosive you can make, he could do it. His fascination with teeth led him to make a tiny explosive that could be hidden in the gums of his unsuspecting patients. In fear that the rebels would go back on the promise to protect his family, he placed one of these explosives in each one of their mouths as he finished up the dental work they were ordered to have."

Déjà said, "Unfucking believable, and what do you mean he ratted you out?"

Amir said, "We'll get back to that later, Little One," then he showed her some more documents from his Blackberry. It was a set of bank accounts in Déjà and Chocolate's names with an amount that Déjà knew she didn't have, and then he showed it to Chocolate. Chocolate's smart ass asked if she could have a debit card to that account. That made Amir smile. He said, "Well, it certainly seems as if the Mandingo Warrior is looking out for his family's future. You see every time you make a mortgage payment, that payment is then deposited into these bank accounts in your names." He looked over at his sister. "Did you know about this, sis?" She just rolled her eyes. "So many secrets, Solomon," Amir said, then he sat back down.

He said, "The other day when I was listening in on your conversation, I heard the Mandingo Warrior outside telling you the story of Charlene, but I was called away before I could hear the end of it. I walked away at the part where he realized she was pregnant." He looked at Déjà's father.

"Such a touching story. But it was riddled with lies. However, I would love to hear the end of it."

Déjà said, "I'll tell you if you explain how my dad ratted you out to save himself."

"Deal," Amir replied. "It's simple: when I realized the rebels had killed your mom, I broke into the Mandingo Warrior's office safe and set off all the tiny bombs he placed in their gums. Instead of escaping with me from the remaining rebels, the Mandingo Warrior made a deal with the US Government for the technology and a new identity in America in exchange for me."

Déjà said, "You're still keeping secrets. What's so special about you that the US government would want you, and why would the US government give a rat's ass about dead African rebels? You're leaving something out."

"So smart, Little One," Amir said, "but some things are better left alone; however, there is still the matter of my bag."

Déjà looked over at her supposed mother and said, "But why did you kill all those innocent rebels when it was your wicked sister that killed my mother and tried to kill me?"

This information sent Amir into a rage. He paced back and forth across the floor. He said, "What is this foolishness you speak, Little One; who told you this madness?"

She said, "It's true; she's crazy just like you."

Blue Eyes

He sat back down and took some deep breaths. It seemed like he was having trouble breathing. He reached into his jacket pocket and pulled out an asthma inhaler and took a puff.

Suddenly Déjà's mother had a voice. "Brother, you need to calm down; you never could control your temper and you know it triggers your asthma."

There was a silence in the room. Déjà looked over at her dad, who was giving her that look all parents give their kids that means shut the hell up.

Amir regained his composure and said, "Little One, tell me what you know of your mother's death."

Déjà replied, "Nothing" and put her head down.

Amir walked over to her father. He put his gun to his head. "Tell me what you know or Mandingo Warrior is going to be reunited with Charlene sooner than expected," then he took the safety off. Déjà knew he wasn't playing so she sang like a bird and told the entire story her dad told her. Amir was furious; the thought of his sister murdering the woman he loved bought him to tears. He grabbed his sister by the throat and said, "Why would you do this horrible thing? You knew I loved her; you knew she was my only friend."

She was cold as ice with her reply. "I hated that American whore. She came into my life and stole the love of both the men I loved, my husband and my brother. You expected me to treat her as part of my family. I descended from royalty; she was a lowly American. I considered her

209

garbage."

Déjà thought he was going to choke the life out of her. Déjà started screaming, "No, no, no, don't kill her, please no."

Amir let her go. He stepped back, pulled out his gun and pointed it at his sister. He said, "You've always been an evil, hateful, self-centered bitch," and he shot at her. The bullet hit her leg and she doubled over in pain.

Déjà started screaming and crying; she knew what she told him set him off. She screamed, "Okay, I'll tell you where your bag is." Déjà thought to herself that if he was crazy enough to shoot his sister, he surely wouldn't hesitate to kill all of them once he got his bag. She remembered that Chocolate had left her backpack upstairs in her bathroom. She put it behind the tub so none of the kids could get to it. She just had to figure out how she was going to get upstairs. Then she remembered her menstrual cycle from hell. She asked Amir if he could untie her so she could go to the bathroom. She said she didn't understand why he had her hands tied anyway, since he and his associates were the ones holding the guns and she and Chocolate and Chocolate's niece were just innocent women. Plus, she added, what would her real mother think about him tying her only daughter up and holding her at gunpoint?

Amir motioned for her to shhh. He had his associates untie the ladies, except for his sister, who looked like she was about to pass out from bleeding. He even allowed Déjà to hold the little dog in her lap. Déjà convinced him to bandage his sister up to stop the bleeding. He was confused about Déjà's concern about her. He asked Déjà why she was so concerned about her when she had been nothing but evil toward her. Déjà simply replied, "Because she is my brother's mother and I love him more than you can imagine. And if you kill her, he is going to be destroyed and possibly blame me."

Amir couldn't seem to relate to the brother-sister love they shared but agreed not to kill her. He looked at Déjà and said, "Little One, there are far worse things than death, I assure you."

Déjà just looked at him. She sure as hell didn't want an example. She said, "Now can I go to the bathroom?" She grabbed Chocolate's little cousin and said, "She has to go, too."

Amir motioned his associates to take Déjà to the downstairs bathroom. Déjà had to get to the upstairs bathroom. She said, "No, I need to go upstairs to my personal bathroom, please."

Amir looked puzzled. "What's the difference? A toilet is a toilet."

Déjà could see he was growing impatient and the possibility of him killing her and them all wasn't just a possibility. Déjà gave him the evil eye, then she reached under her skirt, squatted and pulled out her bloody tampon. As she swung it in the air, she said, "Because my personals are upstairs and as you can see, I need them."

Déjà's father just hung his head down in disgust and shook it back in forth. Amir seemed to get a big kick out of this disgusting display. He smiled and said, "Yes, you are your mother's daughter; that was very distasteful but something your mother would do." He said, "Okay upstairs you go, Little One, but please make sure you wash your hands."

Blue Eyes

As his associate led them upstairs, Déjà saw the skateboard Chocolate's little cousin was sliding down the railing with. The associate checked out the bathroom and told Déjà she had two minutes, then he said, "Like the boss said, make sure you wash your hands," and he wrinkled his nose up at her. He insisted that she leave a crack in the door.

Déjà replied, "Why, so you can see and smell the blood?"

The thought of that made him sick to his stomach. He made a gagging motion and closed the door. He said, "You got three minutes."

Quickly Déjà grabbed the backpack. She told Chocolate's niece, "Do you think you can ride the skateboard through the window and get help?"

Chocolate's niece replied sarcastically, "Of course, if I don't die from all the glass falling on me and possibly stabbing me in the heart," then she looked at Déjà in disbelief.

Déjà replied as she was holding up Chocolate's guns and strapping one to her body, "I mean after I shot the window out?" The thought of shooting her window out made her cringe.

The niece looked afraid. Déjà said, "It's the only way. You see he is crazy; he shot his associate and killed him, then he shot his sister--now you tell me what he might do to people he don't even know?"

The associate knocked on the door and said, "Time's up. Wash your hands and come along."

Blue Eyes

Déjà looked at the girl. :It's now or never."

The girl said, "But what if I don't make it?"

Déjà reminded her of how she insisted she was the skateboard queen. That seemed to pump her up. She said, "Yeah auntie, I really am the shit!"

Déjà pinched her. "Watch your mouth, girl," then Déjà said, "Ok here we go." At that moment Déjà was thanking God for Chocolate's obsession with guns! She opened the door and shot the associate in the head without hesitation. Chocolate always told her, "If you gon' pull the gun out make sure you down to squeeze the trigger." Although Déjà wasn't a killer, she sure as hell wasn't going to be killed. He hit the floor and she and the girl ran straight to the stairs. The girl went straight to work on her skateboard. Déjà stopped at the top of the steps and unloaded the gun on the window. The girl, the skateboard , and the little dog went flying through it to get help.

When Déjà got downstairs she saw that her dad had one of the associates in what looked like some wrestling move. He had his head between his thighs and looked like he was going to squeeze the life out of him. He told Déjà to shoot but she froze when she saw Amir holding a gun to her father's head.

He told Déjà, "Just give me my bag, Little One, and I'll walk away," but before Déjà could answer she heard police sirens. Amir hit Déjà's dad in the head with the gun once again and walked over to Déjà. She pointed the gun at him. He said, "Little One, I know you would never shoot me because you know that I love you and your mother, but this ain't over."

And he simply walked out the door and disappeared.

Déjà couldn't bring herself to shoot him. She knew in her heart he loved her and she knew he had more secrets to tell, possibly that he was her real dad. The sirens were getting closer. Déjà tried to untie her dad but he insisted she didn't and he told her, "When the police get here don't say a word. Let me do all the talking." Déjà was fine with that shit; she wouldn't know where to begin telling the police what happen.

When the police got there they observed the scene, treated Déjà's so-called mom and bandaged her gunshot wound up. The EMTs said it was just a flesh wound and that she would live. They transported Déjà's father in the helicopter to the hospital. Déjà and Chocolate refused treatment they both insisted they were fine. Chocolate's niece went to the hospital for some minor glass scratches.

Déjà kept looking around for Amir but he was nowhere in sight. Déjà thought it seemed odd that police weren't pressuring them for answers; they just removed the bodies from the house and walked around taking notes. Then Déjà saw a familiar face. It was The Chief. He took Déjà in the room and said, "We are going to discuss every last detail of this later, but right now keep your mouth shut and only talk to this lawyer," and he introduced her to the lawyer. After it was all said and done, The Chief came and told Déjà that her dad was fine; he just had a few bumps and bruises. He was going to get some X-rays and more than likely would be released. Déjà's father insisted that Déjà and Chocolate check into a hotel. The Chief took them to the hotel suite he and Déjà stayed at. Déjà knew he was pissed. He told Déjà, "I can't help you if you lie to me."

Blue Eyes

Déjà told him the whole story. She lied and said she gave Amir the bag because she knew The Chief was going to insist she give it to him. Déjà was curious about the contents of that bag because she had a feeling that Amir wouldn't go through all that trouble to recover a few hundred thousand dollars, plus he never explained why the US government would want him so badly.

That next morning Chocolate was kind of quiet. She seemed to be off in deep thought. Déjà knew she was thinking about what happened last night and she was also still thinking about Otis. Déjà didn't try to comfort her; she figured that was something Chocolate was going to have to work out on her own. Déjà got a call from her dad that he was home and all right. He told her not to come to the house and not to go to hers until he made a few calls. Déjà tried to ask him about the accusation Amir had made against him, but he wasn't having it, He asked to speak to The Chief. Before she handed The Chief the phone she said, "You have worked on my and Chocolate's mouths for years. Maybe you planted an explosive in our gums?"

He responded, "Maybe so; in that cause you should watch how you speak to me."

Déjà was shocked. She had never heard her dad speak like that. She knew he was on one. She handed The Chief the phone, and after he spoke to The Chief he hung up without even saying goodbye to Déjà. She knew he was pissed at her because she didn't shoot Amir and that she had spoke freely with Amir about personal things. But Déjà couldn't worry about that right now; she couldn't get through to Chagita in Mexico.

Blue Eyes

Déjà and Chocolate were waiting for the okay from the LAPD to leave the country. They finally received clearance to leave a week later. LAPD said they got a tip from a Russian lady that the same Russian man they found dead in Déjà's house had held her in a motel room for three days. The police told Déjà and Chocolate that they were very lucky they fought back 'cause they could be in some foreign country right now as sex slaves. Chocolate and Déjà knew it was the same lady that Chocolate had saved in the motel room. Déjà could tell The Chief was pissed at her but at the same time he was still in love with her, which was hard for Déjà because she loved him and Ghost.

At the time neither one of them were pressuring her. The Chief had flown back up north and Ghost was settling into his new apartment. There was no word from Amir. Lucas was back from Cambodia and Déjà was able to return to her house. She had a maid service clean it from top to bottom. She decided she was going to sell it and buy another one, but being the businesswoman that she was, she rethought that and decided to rent it out. She loved that house but didn't want to live there anymore.

Foxy and the little dog seemed to being getting along. But just like two bitches, they fought every now and then. Chocolate and Déjà decided not to even go near the money bag until they were sure Amir was gone, although they were curious about it. Déjà insisted that when they were counting the money they missed something. Déjà had a strange feeling that somebody was still watching her but she wasn't scared; she knew it was Amir. It seemed strange that after all the horrible things she knew he had done, after all her father's warnings to stay away from him, she still wasn't afraid of him. She had questions and he had the answers and she was going to get them or he was never going to get his hands on the bag.

216

Chapter Thirteen

Heart to Heart

Heart to Heart

After Déjà convinced her father that she would be safe with Chocolate in Mexico and promised not to have any contact with Amir under any circumstances, she and Chocolate were off to the airport. Déjà's father insisted they fly, saying that when traveling through Mexico driving was not an option. As they boarded the plane Déjà got a text from an unfamiliar number that read,

"Don't worry; you're going to be safe in Mexico. I'm always watching." Déjà knew immediately it was from Amir. She looked around the airport but there was no sign of him. When she tried to call the number back it was disconnected and all attempts to text it back failed. Déjà said a prayer before the plane took off. The flight was less than an hour but seemed like days!

Déjà was praying the entire time and watching Chocolate. It seemed like Chocolate was taking this hard; she was breaking down more and more. When they got off the plane they were greeted by John Paul, who took them to a remote little hospital outside of town. He said he had Luscious flown to a private hospital so she could get the best of care, as well as her boyfriend and Chagita. When they entered the hospital Déjà saw Luscious' boyfriend's mother in the waiting room holding some strange object but Déjà dared not ask her what it was. Déjà could see she had her private nurse there, too. Déjà asked John Paul how they got there and he said Luscious' boyfriend's lawyer had them flown down.

They couldn't see Luscious right away. They didn't know what the hell was going on. The hospital was very quiet and what talking they did hear was in Spanish. Luscious' mom was in the room with Luscious.

Finally the nurse motioned for John Paul and said that he, Déjà and

Heart to Heart

Chocolate could visit Luscious but only for a little while, as after her heart transplant she was very weak and should not be upset.

Déjà eyes grew big as marbles. She looked at John Paul and said, "What the hell is she talking about?"

John Paul said he would explain everything later, "But for right now, please don't upset Luscious and whatever she says, just agree with her, because she is a little confused now." When she got stronger he would tell her the entire story.

Chocolate was pissed. She said, "What the fuck? I'm so fucking tired of hearing stories. I don't give a fuck what happened; as long as this bitch is breathing I'm good, so keep your fucking story to yourself!" Then she pushed her way past both of them and went in the room.

Déjà walked in behind her. Luscious was lying there in deep thought. She smiled when she saw Déjà and Chocolate and said, "What took you Heffa's so long? Bitches, I could have died." Then she smiled again.

Déjà replied, "It's a long story. I would tell you but Chocolate isn't in the mood for stories." Then she looked over at Chocolate and stuck her tongue out at her. Chocolate rolled her eyes at Déjà and sat in the chair.

The ladies talked for a while, then Luscious looked like she was going to cry. She said, "You know what he told me in the car, right before the crash?"

Déjà assumed she was talking about her producer boyfriend since he was the only man in the car with them. "No sweetie, what did he say?"

Luscious looked at Déjà she said, "He said he loved me; that I stole his heart and no matter what I'll always have it."

"Aww, sweetie that's beautiful," Déjà replied. Chocolate just frowned; she hated mushy-mellow dramatic stuff.

Then Luscious said, "Well, I guess it's just fate that I really will always have his heart, since it's his heart inside my body that's keeping me alive."

With that said, Chocolate just got up and left the room, mumbling, "Aw hell naw, I don't even fucking wanna know!"

Déjà was confused. She looked over at John Paul, who didn't say a word; he just looked off into space, as if he didn't hear what she said. Déjà said, "Sweetie, what are you talking about?"

Luscious told Déjà that the nurses told her that the man who donated his heart to her told them that he loved her very much, even though he really didn't get a chance to spend a lot of time with her. She said that the nurses bought her all her boyfriend's personal items and said they had notified his next of kin. At that point Luscious teared up. Then she held out her wrist to show Déjà his watch she had been wearing since the nurses gave her his items. She told Déjà that she'd never loved anybody like she loved him and that she felt they were soul mates. She told Déjà that the universe had brought him to her and that it was divine power working with them. She asked how else could his heart be a perfect match for her? She said the odd thing was that she could somehow still feel his spirit.

Heart to Heart

Déjà sure as hell didn't want to hear all Luscious' voodoo bullshit right now. So she said, "Sweetie, I'm going to check on Chagita now. You let your new heart get some rest now."

John Paul wouldn't even look at Déjà. He pulled Chocolate and Déjà to the side and said he wanted to talk to them about something. Déjà told him she knew all about what went down with Chagita and his father and that she knew exactly who he was. She told him all about what Chagita said his father told her. John Paul told Déjà to sit down because although all she said was true, his father left out some parts of his story. Déjà told John Paul she didn't want to hear it because she had been through enough bullshit the last few months and she was going to crack if anything else happened. John Paul assured her that she wasn't going to crack; she was strong but she had to hear him out because he was going to need her help if Luscious didn't make it. The thought of Luscious not making it sent Déjà into a frenzy. She had to pull herself back together to listen to John Paul.

He said, "Long years ago when I was a boy, my father used to fly to the States. He loved to go to New Orleans to eat; he loved the culture down there. He met a young beautiful African American woman, they had an affair, and she got pregnant. He tried to make her have an abortion but she refused. He sent his men to take her out but something went terribly wrong and both his men ended up blowing their brains out." He said when his dad went to take her out himself he felt something evil--more evil than him--working through the woman. He said she spoke in a tongue he'd never heard, then something seemed to take over her body and threaten to kill him if he laid one hand on her and the unborn child. He was so scared of her he left New Orleans, never to return again.

Heart to Heart

"However, he didn't know that my mom had been in contact with this lady." He said his mom warned her that his dad was evil. He said later he found out that what his dad witnessed was some voodoo trick the lady had done. He said as for the two men his dad sent to take the lady out, he couldn't explain their actions. He continued to say that his mom provided for the lady and her child and kept them away from his dad for years, until she took her own life. He stopped and looked up at Déjà. He said, "When my mom died it was my responsibility to provide for them. I moved the lady and her daughter to Long Beach, California, next to a young girl I also was responsible for."

Déjà's eyes got big as marbles Chocolate just shook her head. "Oh my God," were the first words that came out of Déjà's mouth. "Luscious is that little girl and Chagita is the other." Déjà just stared off into space.

"Yes," John Paul replied, "she's my half sister. She and her mother have been my responsibility ever since my mother died. Luscious' mother knows all about Chagita. She promised never to say a word, and she told Luscious her father died when she was a baby."

Déjà said, "So what do you need my help with?"

He said, "Well, Luscious needed a heart transplant; without it she was going to die. Her heart couldn't stand another heart attack. So I arranged for her to have a heart with a perfect match."

Déjà replied, "Well, how the hell did you do that? Because buying organs is illegal; they wouldn't let you do that."

Heart to Heart

He looked at Déjà and said, "Well, it may be illegal in the States but look around: we are in Mexico, and anything can be bought and done here if you have the money."

Déjà looked around and they were definitely in Mexico. Déjà said, "Okay, but where did you get the heart and how did you know it was a perfect match for Luscious?"

He said, "From her father."

Déjà squinted her eyes and said, "We both know that's not possible; we both know what happened to him."

Chocolate replied, "What the hell happened to him?"

Déjà looked at Chocolate and said, "You don't wanna know."

John Paul said, "Well, that's where it gets complicated. I know Chagita thought she took him out but that was only because that's what she saw. I followed her that day and after she left I had the doctors revive him. He wasn't dead, just unconscious. I let her believe he was dead because she feared him so. But she had nothing to fear. He was a changed man. He had found the Lord and repented of all his sins. He freely gave his heart to keep his daughter from dying; that alone should get him at least to the gates of heaven."

Déjà blurted out, "You gave my friend a heart of a killer? What the fuck? She's already weird with that voodoo shit; now she's gonna be a psychopath."

Heart to Heart

John Paul said he highly doubted that and it was the only choice he had: either the psychopath's heart or die.

Déjà said, "Well when you put it like that..." Then Déjà said, "But why does she think she has her boyfriend's heart? Why did y'all lie to her?"

John Paul said, "I never lied to her; I just never disagreed with her. She is not strong enough yet to know the truth." He said, "The nurses tried to talk to Luscious but they don't speak English well and Luscious misunderstood what they said but what they told her seemed to make her wanna live, so I just rolled with it."

Déjà agreed but told him before she left the hospital, he better tell her the truth. Déjà then asked about Luscious' boyfriend. John Paul said Luscious' boyfriend had some serious injuries; however, the doctors expected him to make a full recovery. He said he was a few rooms down but he wasn't strong enough to move yet. He said he was going to need intense therapy. But he was alive and in his right state of mind.

Déjà and Chocolate went to visit downstairs with Chagita, who was perfectly fine except for her broken leg and arm. She had a few scratches on her face which she had already started putting cream on. Who knew Chagita was so dramatic? They had a good visit with Chagita. She said John Paul had already explained to her what happened and that she was relieved that she wasn't a killer after all. She said she loved Luscious, no matter whose heart she had. She referred to Luscious as her new sister–in–law and held up her hand to show her engagement ring. She said John Paul asked her to marry him; that's why they were going to Tijuana, to have drinks and celebrate.

Heart to Heart

After a few weeks in the hospital in Mexico, Luscious' mother, who was pissed with John Paul but grateful he saved her daughter's life, took Luscious home to recover. They told Luscious the story; oddly, she wasn't upset. She was overjoyed her boyfriend was still alive. They both stayed at his house and had around the clock nurses and maid service. Luscious was getting stronger every day and working harder on her lingerie line, which Déjà had to admit was turning out nice: hot, steamy and sexy, with just a little touch of elegance.

Chagita was back at work with those kids whom she seemed to love; she said they kept her strong. Déjà was in her new house with her new dog Foxy and the little dog. She was still seeing Ghost and having weekly conversations with The Chief. Déjà's dad had moved into Déjà's old house. He said he wasn't uncomfortable there; hell, he said had seen worse things happen in his country.

Déjà was reflecting on what happened, all the lies that had been told all the secrets that had been kept. Two things stuck out in her mind. The first thing was Soni Lynn's mom Mary threatening the wicked witch of Baldwin hills and her dad mentioning that her real mom Charlene had an aunt named Suga Bell--which just so happen to be Soni Lynn's grandmothers name? Plus, Déjà remembered at the anniversary party how the little girl asked her if she and Soni Lynn's mom Mary were sisters because they looked alike. Déjà pulled Soni Lynn's social media page up and started looking at all her pictures of her mother. Déjà thought to herself that the little girl was right; they did look alike and they could pass for sisters.

Déjà got on the phone and called Soni Lynn and told her they needed to

226

talk. Soni Lynn agreed to meet her later that day at her new house. She also said she was going to bring her mother with her. As Déjà was getting dressed she received a text that read, "If you truly believe that I loved your mother and you, please meet me at this location and bring my bag." Déjà knew it was Amir, and today she was going to get some answers. She finished getting dressed and went to the place where she and Chocolate hid the bag and then made her way to the address Amir gave her. As she drove up into this Beverly Hills mansion, she took a good look around. All she saw was the even bigger mansion across the street. Déjà started laughing to herself. She thought, *Why don't white folks ever put curtains up? You can see straight through their houses,* then she proceeded to the door.

Amir greeted her at the door. Déjà looked him up and down. He seemed to be more handsome than she remembered. She was getting a good look at him to see if she resembled him in any way; hell as far, as she knew, with all the secrets her family kept, he could possibly be her dad.

"Hey Little One, good to see you. You look beautiful, as always," he said.

She replied, "Yeah, yeah, cut the bullshit, Mister and let's get straight to the point. Are you my dad? I brought you your bag and I didn't call the police, so the least you can do is tell me the truth."

He looked at her; it appeared that he enjoyed seeing her all fired up. He smiled and said, "Thank you for my bag, I really appreciate that. I wasn't worried about you calling the cops. I knew you wouldn't; even after the Mandingo Warrior warned you not to go near me, I knew you would still come. You have your mother's spunk and energy.

"Once again, cut the bullshit and answer the fucking question," Déjà replied.

Amir frowned and said, "That's the only thing I didn't particularly care for about your mother. She cursed like a sailor--such a nasty habit for a beautiful woman."

Déjà smacked her lips. He said, "And to answer your question, no Little One, I'm not your father. Unfortunately, the Mandingo Warrior is your father for certain; I never touched your mother although I desired her greatly. I never got the opportunity; when she came to me she was already pregnant with you and sex with a pregnant lady is not my thing."

Déjà said, "Way too much information" and they both started laughing. He asked Déjà to stay and have lunch with him. Déjà agreed. She had more questions. She wanted to know what he knew about this Suga Bell lady. He told her all he knew was that she was her mom's aunt and that her mom loved her very much and spent summers with her in New York. He prepared a feast and they ate, talked and drank wine. He told Déjà stories of her mother, something Déjà's father was never going to do. The very thought of her mother brought Déjà's father to tears. Amir seemed to be a pretty cool dude.

After they ate, Amir told Déjà to come to the balcony; he wanted to show her something. As Déjà went out on the balcony, she noticed what looked like a rifle carrier. He gave her some binoculars and said, "Look into that window" and pointed across the street to the bigger mansion. Déjà looked through the binoculars to see a young man asleep. He had what looked like an IV drip attached to him. And a lady was sitting in the chair reading a magazine. When the lady put the magazine down, she was Déjà's stepmom.

Déjà got nervous. She looked at the rifle, then at Amir, and said, "Are you crazy? That's your sister; you can't kill her. Please, she's my brother's mother."

Amir smiled and said, "I'm not going to kill the wicked witch of Baldwin Hills ,Little One; I've told you there are far worse things than death"

Déjà said, "Well, why are you spying on her?"

He said, "Aren't you curious why she is over there?"

Déjà replied, "No, she is a doctor; sometimes she has private clients."

He said, "I know this, but do you ever wonder what she does for them?"

"No," Déjà said, "because I know she watches them after surgery."

Amir smiled. "So she says." Then Déjà heard sirens and saw police cars pull into the driveway at the mansion across the street. The police presence didn't seem to bother Amir at all. He said, "Little One, do you remember when the king of pop died? Remember the doctor who gave him the fatal dose of medicine?" Déjà just looked; she didn't say a word. Amir continued, "Well, for some time that same medicine has been missing from the medicine cabinet where the wicked witch of Baldwin hills happens to be an anesthesiologist who has unlimited access to it."

Déjà put her head down and said, "Please don't tell me she's been stealing it and using it for her rich, over-privileged clients."

Amir smiled. "No, no Little One, she's way too sophisticated to do such a thing; however, I'm not." He said, "All her life she's been a spoiled, self-centered, rotten bitch, and today she is going to get what's coming to her." He said he arranged for the medicine to come up missing and for it to be found not only at her client's house but in his system. He said to the wicked witch of Baldwin Hills, her reputation and appearance were everything and today he was going to ruin both. He said, "That spiteful little bitch is going to wish she was dead."

Déjà looked on as she saw the police drag her mom out, screaming and hollering in handcuffs. Amir snapped a few pictures of her and said he was going to post them on social media and tag her in them so all her uppity friends and colleagues could see. He said the shame of it all would ruin her. He looked at Déjà he said, "And that, Little One, is one of those things worse than death, especially to the wicked witch of Baldwin hills."

Déjà had to admit that she didn't feel sorry for her. After all the police had left and everything calmed down, Déjà asked Amir what was in that bag that was so important to him, because she definitely knew it wasn't the money.

Amir smiled he said, "If I tell you, I would have to kill you."

Déjà said, "I don't think that's funny at all-wrong timing!" She walked over to him and said, "You're never going to tell me, are you?"

"Nope," he replied.

She said, "So now what? You disappear and continue to spy on me and Chocolate?"

"Yep," he said, "but first I want to give you something." He pulled out a ring box and said, "The day Mandingo Warrior came and tricked your mom into taking him back, I had gone to pick this up." He handed Déjà the box. He said, "I was going to ask her to marry me but I was too late; she said she was in love with your father. She also said she loved me too but loved him more. She refused to even open the box."

Déjà felt bad for Amir; she could see he was heartbroken over her real mom and that he truly loved her. Déjà opened the ring box. She said, "It's absolutely beautiful." It was a blue diamond surrounded by white diamonds.

He said, "I chose that rare blue diamond because of the nickname she gave me. She called me 'blue eyes.'" Then he removed the sunglasses he always wore and said, "The one thing I always hated about myself was the one thing she loved about me; she said they gave me character."

Déjà laughed she said, "Yeah, you are a character, one like I've never known."

Déjà turned around to see him staring at her. She knew he was wishing she was her mom and longing for her. Déjà walked up to him. She wasn't totally convinced that he was telling the truth about not being her dad. She decided to try to kiss him; if he was her father she knew he would never allow it. She got closer to him. She could tell it made him a little uneasy. She put his hands around her waist and leaned in to kiss him. To her surprise, he grabbed a tight grip on her and followed through with the kiss. He kissed her like he had been wanting to do that for a long time. After the kiss he held her close to him. He said softly, "I'm not your father."

Déjà replied softly, "I'm not her either."

He squeezed Déjà one more time and gently pushed her away. He said sadly, "I know."

Déjà backed up. The tension was thick. Déjà said jokingly, "Well, technically I am her. I mean I'm her daughter; I was inside her body from the day she was born so yeah, technically I am her." Then she smiled

Amir laughed and said, "Well okay, when you put it like that, I guess so." He said, "Please forgive me, Little One, I would never take advantage of you. It was a moment of weakness; you look so much like her it's irresistible."

Déjà smiled and said, "I know. I can understand your attraction to all this, but I'm not offended I kissed you. But it will never happen again; it's not me you were kissing in your mind, it was Charlene."

He smiled. He said, "Little One, speaking of kissing, what are you going to do about these two gentlemen you are stringing along--The Chief and your young lover?"

Déjà replied, "So nosy, aren't you?"

Heart to Heart

He said, "Well, my fatherly advice would be to go with The Chief. He is more stable, more your age and would make a proper husband for you, but on the other hand I like the young lover. He's ambitious, goes for what he wants, and you seem to be happier when he's around." He said, "So I guess I'm team young lover."

Déjà started cracking up laughing and hugged him goodbye. As she drove off, he ran to the car and said, "Oh yeah, Little One--stay off the pole. Very unladylike."

Chapter Fourteen

Family Ties

Family Ties

Déjà forgot all about her meeting with Soni Lynn and her mother Mary. It really didn't matter, since Amir had answered all her questions about her real mom. Déjà was convinced that Soni Lynn's mom would answer the rest. A few days later she met up with them for lunch. Déjà brought Chocolate and her dad for support. The wicked witch of Baldwin hills was still in police custody, which didn't even matter to Déjà's dad or Déjà.

Soni Lynn and her mom were already having appetizers when they got there. As soon as Deja's father saw Mary he was taken with her. Déjà pinched him and whispered in his ear that she was married to a killer. That didn't seem to detour him. "Hell," he replied, "so am I."

Déjà laughed then said, "Way too soon to be making jokes, Mandingo." They both smiled.

Mary apologized for her mom Suga Bell not being there. She said Suga Bell recently had elective upper eyelid surgery, which was a simple in and out procedure; however, Suga Bell was acting like she had major surgery so she flew back home so her husband could take care of her. She said she would meet Déjà when she recovered. Soni Lynn started laughing and said, "Hot mess."

Mary explained that Déjà's real mom Charlene was Suga Bell's niece and that Charlene's mom Liza, who was Suga Bell's oldest sister, asked Mary to find her on her wedding day. Mary explained to them that she found Déjà through a friendly source she had working in the Federal Bureau of Investigations. She said she sent Soni Lynn in to try to get a feel for what Déjà was like and to see what she already knew about her biological mom. Mary assured Déjà's dad that she wasn't going to say a word to her without his permission and that if after she spoke with him he didn't want her to know about them, she would respect his wishes. She said the scene at the anniversary was just acoincidence; nevertheless, it was a blessing to her family because now they had the opportunity to meet Déjà. Mary told Déjà that if she didn't want to pursue a relationship with her family that they would understand; however, they would love to welcome her into their family.

Déjà felt an instant connection with Mary, sort of like the big sister she never had. They enjoyed lunch and Mary told Déjà, Chocolate, and Déjà's father all about her family. Mary asked Déjà's father if it was too late for the wicked witch of Baldwin Hills to go to jail for the murder of Déjà's mother and he said that there was nothing that they could do because the federal government gave her asylum for that crime when they entered the States; that was part of the deal he made with them. But Déjà assured them that her shame of being accused of being a drug dealer was way worse to her than her going to prison.

Mary took a liking to Chocolate and told her she was going to have her best friend Katy, who was an excellent lawyer, look into the situation with Otis. She said that it was very unusual for a prison not to release information to an inmate's wife. Soni Lynn, who was going to be working this summer as a paralegal, offered to help her also. After they ate they exchanged numbers and emails.

Soni Lynn continued on as an intern for Déjà, and Déjà's relationship with Ghost was developing into something serious: they were going away on a weekend trip together. Déjà was truly looking forward to that because everybody knows that vacation sex is the bomb.com.

Family Ties

The wicked witch of Baldwin Hills finally got released on bail and the judge put her on house arrest until further notice. This was even more humiliating for her. She also got fired from her job at the hospital. Everything was settling down.

Déjà was over at Mama Pearly's house. She went to go check on the pregnant teenager; during all the confusion in her life, that had slipped her mind. They sat in Mama Pearly's formal living room, which was totally off limits to everybody and exceptionally uncomfortable because all the furniture was covered in this thick plastic that stuck to you when it was hot. Déjà choose to talk to her in there because she knew it was private. The teenager sat down. Déjà looked at her. There was no sign of her being pregnant at all. The teenager rubbed her hand over her stomach so Déjà could see it was flat. Déjà said, "What happened?"

As she started to answer Déjà saw the teenager's mother standing in the door way. The teenager couldn't see her because the chair she was sitting in was facing Déjà. Déjà didn't reveal that her mother was behind her. She wanted her to hear what her daughter was saying. The teenager said, "I had an abortion."

Déjà said, "Okay, that's your choice, but why?"

She said she had had an abortion because she felt all alone. She said the boy's parents refused to have anything to do with the baby and they sent him down South to get away from her. She said her mom was too busy getting high and that she knew she wasn't going to help her. "Hell," she said, "my little brother misses half his therapy sessions because Mama is too lazy to walk him five blocks to the therapy session." She continued to say that it was the best thing for her to do.

Déjà said, "Where did you get the money for the abortion?"

The teenager said she got the money from her grandfather, Mr. Johnson, and that he took her and waited on her both days. She said she was so far along she had to have a two-day procedure. After she said that, she told Déjà that Mr. Johnson and Mama Pearly had been so good to her and that without them she didn't know what she would do or where she would be. She said she was scheduled to take the SAT this Saturday and that whatever school accepted her and gave her a full scholarship, she was going. She said she wanted to get as far away from her mother as possible and that she had never felt anything but contempt for her mother because of the way she treated her and her little brother.

After the teenager's mother heard that, tears rolled down her face and she walked away. Déjà never mentioned to the teenager that her mother was standing behind her. Déjà hugged the teenager and reminded her to be careful and not to let this happen again.

Déjà found the teenager's mother in Mama Pearly's room on the computer. She looked at Déjà and said, "I'm a terrible mother, Chunky. I need my ass beat."

Déjà said, "Well yes, you have been a terrible mother but what are you going to do about it?"

She said after listening to her baby she promised she was going to rehab and get herself together. She and Déjà made plans for Déjà to drop her off the following Monday when Déjà returned from her weekend get-away with Ghost. That was another situation Déjà had to deal with, but when she tried to explain to Chocolate's other aunt about her and Ghost, Chocolate's aunt told her she couldn't care less; that Déjà was always going to come first, before any man, and that if Ghost made her happy, she should do the damn thing. That's what Déjà loved about Chocolate's aunts; they always had some snappy saying.

Everyone was sitting on the porch talking to Mama Pearly and enjoying each other's company. Chocolate was in the kitchen frying chicken with her daughter, who was down for the week. Déjà saw Soni Lynn's car pull up, which wasn't a big deal; over the weeks they'd gotten really close. But what was a big deal was her passenger.

He got out of the car. He looked around and said, "Hey y'all" and gave Mama Pearly a big hug and squeeze. He said, "I really missed you, lady."

Mama Pearly couldn't believe her eyes. She said, "Otis, how?" She couldn't even talk; she just put her arms around him and started thanking God for the blessing.

He held Mama Pearly's hand and said, "I'm so sorry I wasn't here for you during your difficult time. I prayed for the Lord to give you and me strength to get through it. I know there's nothing I could say to make you feel better, but always know I love you like you're my mother and I loved Chocolate with all my heart, and my daughter--I still can't believe it."

Déjà came off the porch and interrupted that conversation. She could tell by the look on Mama Pearly's face she was confused. Soni Lynn whispered to Déjà that she didn't have time to tell him that Chocolate wasn't dead, or their daughter (that's why Otis tore the cell up, the correction officer told him Chocolate and their daughter died in a car crash.). She said he didn't say a word in the car; he just insisted she take him directly to Mama Pearly's house. She said he was big and scary, plus he looked dangerous, so she just got here as quickly as she could. She said it was the longest ride of her life.

When Otis saw Déjà he grabbed her and hugged her. He just started crying and begging for her forgiveness. He said he should have been there for them. Déjà was trying to calm him down so she could tell him that Chocolate and their daughter O'Shay were fine, but he was inconsolable.

By that time somebody had run and gotten Chocolate and O'Shay. Chocolate was just standing on the porch looking at him. O'Shay ran to him, screaming, "Daddy!" Otis stood there like he was frozen. He didn't move; he just stared at O'Shay in disbelief. She almost knocked him down hugging him. He cried tears of joy and when Chocolate stepped off the porch, he dropped to his knees in prayer. Déjà had never seen him cry. Otis, O'Shay and Chocolate all stood there hugging and crying.

Later Chocolate explained to him all that happened. She said that the Russian paid the lady corrections officer to tell him she and O'Shay had died in a car crash just to fuck with him because he was upset about her slicing his private parts. The part about him being gay and in love with his cellmate was the correctional officer's idea to hurt Chocolate. Chocolate said a few days ago Otis' cellmate stopped by the house. He said after Otis tore up the cell they put Otis in solitary confinement. He said they took him to the mental hospital, saying he tried to hang himself, but that was an absolute lie. The cellmate said when they first put him in Otis' cell he was scared; everyone said Otis was a killer and homophobic. He said Otis was cool; he just told him not to bring none of that gay shit in his cell. The cellmate said the last time he saw him was when they dragged him off to solitary confinement. However, he heard about what went down from one of the other corrections officers whom he shared a secret with. Chocolate said she didn't even ask him what the secret was. She didn't want to know. Chocolate also said that Otis's cellmate wanted to thank him for protecting him in prison. He said he was truly grateful and that Otis was a stand-up dude. Homophobic, but an otherwise stand-up dude.

Otis just stood there staring at Chocolate. Soni Lynn came down off the porch and said when Otis' lawyer threatened to sue the prison and expose all their secrets and report the female corrections officers for sexual harassment against the male inmates, the prison settled out of court with her and agreed to release Otis and his cell mate if they waived their right to sue and signed a confidentiality agreement. Otis said he would have given his left leg to get out.

Soni Lynn said she didn't tell Chocolate because she wasn't sure if the deal was going to go through or not until this morning, when the prison called her and the lawyer to prepare their client to sign the papers. Otis' cellmate got out earlier because his original crime was fraud and stealing.

Otis started laughing when Chocolate told him what the prison guard told her about him leaving her for his cellmate. He said she was just a hateful, lonely bitch and Chocolate should have known way better than that.

O'Shay spent the night with Déjà. She said she was giving her parents some privacy. Otis insisted she come home first thing in the morning. When he said home, he smiled and a tear rolled down his cheek. Déjà said, "Look here, triple OG, you way too sensitive to be as hard as you claim to be."

He hugged Déjà and said, "Man, freedom is so special I wouldn't jaywalk across the street."

They both smiled. That night Déjà packed up her suitcase for her weekend get-away with Ghost. He showed up with movies and chicken wings. Déjà texted Soni Lynn to coordinate their trip to New York to meet the rest of Déjà's new family.

Déjà smiled to herself as she thought about the family she already had. Hell, Chocolate's family was just as much her family as they were Chocolate's; it didn't matter that Chocolate was the only one related to her by blood. She loved all of them the same. She also had a father and brother who loved her dearly. Now she had Soni Lynn, who was her blood cousin, and they had formed a bond. She and Mary were talking and texting every day, so they were getting close. Plus she had Amir, who she knew would always be around, whether her father liked it or not. She had to admit she did like Amir a lot; he was a pretty cool dude. Plus, she knew he loved her just because he loved her mother. She thought about The Chief every so often but decided to back off; she was happy with Ghost and she wanted to see where that relationship was going to go, and so far so good.

As she finished packing and Ghost put all her bags in the car, she got a text: "Way to go, team young love. I knew he could do it. I love it when the underdog wins. Be safe on your trip. Remember, I'm always watching, Little One." Déjà thought she'd text back, even though she knew Amir wouldn't respond. She wrote, "Always?" To her surprise, he responded in all caps, "ALWAYS" Déjà smiled to herself. She was tempted to text again but she didn't want to push her luck. She knew he was watching and one day she would see him again. She never did figure out what was in that bag that was so important to him but like Amir said, "Some things are better left unknown."

In the car Ghost informed Déjà that they were taking a train ride up the coast and would be stopping in Santa Barbara for the weekend. That sounded nice and relaxing to Déjà; she'd had enough drama for a while. When they got to the train station Ghost went to check in and get the tickets. Déjà decided to make a call and check on Chocolate to make sure she wasn't overwhelmed with the return of Otis. Suddenly she felt her phone drop to the ground. Someone had bumped into her.

"Damn," she said. As she bent down to pick it up she noticed that the screen was cracked again. "Damn," she said out loud. "Shit, I just got this phone fixed."

The gentleman that bumped into her bent down to help her. He said, "Oh, Ms. Lady, please forgive me. I wasn't paying attention." He picked up Deja's phone and handed it to her. Déjà caught his slight African accent right away. She stood up and looked up at him. He was tall, dark, good looking, with tribal marks similar to her dad's. He fixed his sunglasses. He said, "Are you all right?" He took out his wallet and tried to hand Déjà some money.

She shook her head no and said, "No, no, that's not necessary. I have insurance." Then she wrinkled up her nose and looked at her phone and said, "But this is the second time in a few months I cracked the screen."

He looked at her, raised his eyebrows, and made a sad face. He said, "Then maybe you should take the money." They both smiled. Déjà refused.

As he tempted her one more time before he put the money back in his wallet, Déjà noticed the huge gold and diamond watch and bracelet he was wearing. As a matter of fact, she checked him out from head to toe. He was wearing a natural colored cashmere sweater, jeans, dress shoes, and he had on a gold chain with a crucifix filled with diamonds. Damn, he looked good and smelled good, Déjà thought to herself.

She spotted the black bag he was carrying. She smiled to herself; the bag made her think of Amir. The man said, "Let me make it up to you. I'm a freelance photographer/artist. Let me draw a portrait of you. You're such a pretty lady." Then he checked Déjà out from head to toe. He said, "I'm on my way to Detroit on business but when I come back, maybe I could give you a call?" Then he said, "I didn't catch your name" as he handed her a business card.

At that point Ghost walked up and took the card from the man. He said, "Her name is Déjà and I'm Ghost, her man. And you are?" Then Ghost gave Déjà that look that meant she was doing too much.

The stranger smiled and said, "Oh my bad, no disrespect meant" and stuck out his hand to shake Ghost's hand.

Family Ties

"None taken," Ghost replied as he shook his hand.

The man said, "I'm Mustafa." Then he smiled. He looked at Déjà and said, "My dad had a issue with names. He wanted me to have a nice, strong name." Then he removed his sun glasses to reveal his sky blue eyes. He pointed to them and said, "Yeah, genetic defect passed to me by my pops."

Déjà gasped for breath for a second as she just stood there looking at him. She thought to herself, Couldn't be.

Mustafa bid Déjà and Ghost a good day and walked off to his train that was calling for the last boarders. They both watched him walk off, then Ghost handed Déjà Mustafa's business card. Déjà's mouth dropped open when she read the name on the card: "Mustafa Ahmad."